PENGUIN PLAYS

## THE CRUCIBLE
SCREENPLAY

Arthur Miller was born in New York City in 1915 and studied at the University of Michigan. His plays include *All My Sons* (1947), *Death of a Salesman* (1949), *The Crucible* (1953), *A View from the Bridge* and *A Memory of Two Mondays* (1955), *After the Fall* (1963), *Incident at Vichy* (1964), *The Price* (1968), *The Creation of the World and Other Business* (1972), and *The American Clock* (1980). He has also written two novels, *Focus* (1945) and *The Misfits*, which was filmed in 1960, and the text for *In Russia* (1969), *Chinese Encounters* (1979), and *In the Country* (1977), three books of photographs by his wife, Inge Morath. His most recent works are *Timebends*, a memoir (1988), the plays *The Ride Down Mt. Morgan* (1991), *The Last Yankee* (1993), and *Broken Glass*, which won the 1995 Olivier award for best play of the London season, as well as *Homely Girl, a Life* (1995), a collection of stories. He has twice won the New York Drama Critics Circle Award, and in 1949 he was awarded the Pulitzer Prize.

Nicholas Hytner directed the films *The Madness of King George* (1994) and *The Crucible* (1996). His work in the theater includes productions for the Royal Shakespeare Company, the National Theatre in London, and Lincoln Center Theater in New York. He has also directed opera for the English National Opera, the Royal Opera, the Paris Opera, and the Bavarian State Opera in Munich.

# BY ARTHUR MILLER

## DRAMA

The Golden Years
The Man Who Had All the Luck
All My Sons
Death of a Salesman
An Enemy of the People (*adaptation of the play by Ibsen*)
The Crucible
A View from the Bridge
After the Fall
Incident at Vichy
The Price
The American Clock
The Creation of the World and Other Business
The Archbishop's Ceiling
The Ride Down Mt. Morgan
Broken Glass

## ONE-ACT PLAYS

A View from the Bridge, *one-act version, with* A Memory of Two Mondays
Elegy for a Lady (*in* Two-Way Mirror)
Some Kind of Love Story (*in* Two-Way Mirror)
I Can't Remember Anything (*in* Danger: Memory!)
Clara (*in* Danger: Memory!)
The Last Yankee

## OTHER WORKS

Situation Normal
The Misfits (*a cinema novel*)
Focus (*a novel*)
I Don't Need You Anymore (*short stories*)
Theatre Essays
Chinese Encounters (*reportage with Inge Morath photographs*)
In the Country (*reportage with Inge Morath photographs*)
In Russia (*reportage with Inge Morath photographs*)
Salesman in Beijing (*a memoir*)
Timebends (*autobiography*)
Homely Girl, a Life (*short stories*)

## COLLECTIONS

Arthur Miller's Collected Plays (Volumes I and II)
The Portable Arthur Miller
The Theater Essays of Arthur Miller (*Robert Martin, editor*)

## VIKING CRITICAL LIBRARY EDITIONS

Death of a Salesman (*edited by Gerald Weales*)
The Crucible (*edited by Gerald Weales*)

## TELEVISION

Playing for Time

## SCREENPLAYS

The Misfits
Everybody Wins
The Crucible

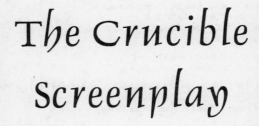

# The Crucible
# Screenplay

ARTHUR MILLER

Penguin Books

PENGUIN BOOKS
Published by the Penguin Group
Penguin Books USA Inc., 375 Hudson Street,
New York, New York 10014, U.S.A.
Penguin Books Ltd, 27 Wrights Lane, London W8 5TZ, England
Penguin Books Australia Ltd, Ringwood, Victoria, Australia
Penguin Books Canada Ltd, 10 Alcorn Avenue,
Toronto, Ontario, Canada M4V 3B2
Penguin Books (N.Z.) Ltd, 182–190 Wairau Road,
Auckland 10, New Zealand

Penguin Books Ltd, Registered Offices:
Harmondsworth, Middlesex, England

*The Crucible* first published in the United States of America by The Viking
Press 1953
This edition published in Penguin Books 1996

10 9 8 7 6 5 4 3 2 1

Color photographs by Barry Wetcher. Black-and-white photographs
by Inge Morath/Magnum.

LIBRARY OF CONGRESS CATALOGING IN PUBLICATION DATA
Miller, Arthur, 1915–
      The crucible: screenplay/Arthur Miller.
          p.   cm.
      ISBN 0 14 02.5909 0 (pbk.)
      I. Miller, Arthur, 1915–   Crucible.   II. Crucible (Motion
picture)   III. Title.
      PN1997.C883   1996
      791.43'72—dc20        96–28139

Printed in the United States of America
Set in Bembo
Designed by Junie Lee

# Note on
# *The Crucible* as Film

## Arthur Miller

Committed to plays since my first writing attempts, I came to believe early in life that film, if it was an art at all rather than a craft, was somehow of a lower order. There were reputed to be a couple of big film masterpieces like *The Birth of a Nation*, which to me seemed like a lot of stupid men rushing around on horseback out in the country somewhere, but in the twenties and thirties, when I was growing up and when film defined itself for me, almost all the films I knew were wonderfully trivial entertainment things that even to my naive mind were obviously aiming to make money with a few laughs or tears or shocks thrown in.

Reading or seeing a play was something else entirely, basically, I suppose, because plays worked away at revealing an *idea*. Movies did not have an idea, they had action. As life became more serious, it was to theater that one looked for some wisdom, and there the prestigious works of centuries existed. (Who even knew the name of a screen writer?) It was the exalted great playwrights who added allure for an ambitious young writer, while it continued to be a strain for me to attribute any real aesthetic aim to film.

But their relative positions in the culture apart, the play is still, I think, a more difficult art to master. For one thing, launched onto the roaring sea of the stage, the play cannot call on other crafts to come to its rescue. There will be no gorgeous horses, no sweet dolphins, no fifty-piece orchestras humming away from four walls of a movie theater to plaster over the cracks in the plot, not to mention actors' faces thirty feet high that can hold even the most wayward moviegoer's attention long after they have by any logic lost the claim to fictive existence. Compared to screenwriting, playwriting is a high-wire act performed over a raging fire below.

I have successfully resisted making screenplays of my plays because the adaptation process most often seems to make less of the original, something I cannot get myself to get enthusiastic about. Worse yet for one about to attempt a screenplay of *The Crucible*, I had over the years developed the prejudice that novels, and in a different way painting, are much more related to film than plays, which after all are propelled by words rather than images. There is also a stronger relation between novels and movies in the way they tell their tales. The film, for example, can gracefully move from place to place, time to time, epoch to epoch in the way a novel does, but a play creaks and groans when forced to do this. Great novels don't necessarily need very much dialogue, but the stage wants to talk, loves the back-and-forth of revealing speech, which is exactly what the movie form seems to inherently resist. The play wants to tell, the movie to show. For some such reason one senses the mustiness of stage scenes that have been shot for film more or less intact. I've often thought this had something to do with tonality; the stage scene is written to be vocally projected onto an audience, a movie scene wants to be overheard.

Confronting the job of adapting *The Crucible*, however, grounded all these interesting, high-flying principles. The initial attraction was that in bursting the bounds of the stage one could move out into the town of Salem, something the play could only infer. My research—almost fifty years earlier—returned to mind, with the testimonies of literally hundreds of folk whose stories had created a marvelously varied tapestry of that seventeenth-century America still in the earliest stages of defining itself. And once I had begun thinking about it as a film, it became obvious that I had in fact always seen it as a flow of images that had had to be evoked through language for the stage.

There was a new excitement in being able to actually show the girls out in the forest with Tituba in the wee hours, playing—as I had always imagined—with the powers of the underworld to bring to life their secret heart's desires. But it was gay, harmless juvenilia, I was sure, until one of them intimated her wish that her former mistress, wife of her beloved John Proctor, might simply die.

There was the possibility of showing the wild beauty of the newly cultivated land bordered by the wild sea, and the utter disorder and chaos of the town meetings where the people were busy condemning one another to death for loving the Evil One. Now one could show the hysteria as it grew rather than for the most part reporting it only.

I had long since come to believe that the more wordless the film the better. But *The Crucible* is founded on words and scenes built on a kind of sculpted language that I feared now to disrupt, for it was obvious that if one didn't want the movie to bear the curse of a static photographed play, one would have to put the play out of mind as much as possible and proceed as though it had never existed. Even so, finding images that would really convey what language had done on the stage was a formidable job. I had taken it to the limits of what seemed possible when luck brought Nick Hytner to me. At first he was incredulous that over a period of three years or more the screenplay had been rejected by at least a dozen of the best American directors. Among its other vicissitudes, it had been the property of a television production company for more than a year, but I managed to break it free when they insisted it could be shot in twenty-two or -three days. (The film took almost two months, and even then was on a very tight schedule.) Hytner went even further than I had, shooting scenes out of doors as much as possible, and in motion from place to place, and utilizing the fantastic Hog Island background and the surrounding sea. But Hytner had had the theatrical background to preserve him from the fear of language, especially archaic-sounding language, which he saw as a strength rather than something from which to flee.

# Filming *The Crucible*

### Nicholas Hytner

We are in the sea. The hysterical villagers swoop down on John Proctor, seize his outstretched arms, and haul him away to prison. Then we cut to a close-up: Abigail Williams, alone in the crowd, the instigator of the hysteria, and now—as she struggles to come to terms with its ruinous consequences for the man she desires—one of its victims.

This insistence on the inseparable link between communal chaos and personal trauma lies at the heart of our transformation of *The Crucible* from play to film. In crude terms, where the theater operates in permanent medium shot, a movie can open wide enough to contain a whole society and move in close enough to see into a girl's heart. More particularly, there is a specifically cinematic energy that crackles in the cut between shots—so that the violence of the mob becomes both the consequence and the source of the pain and confusion behind the eyes of the girl in the close-up. Images feed one another in a spiral of cause and effect that exactly reflects the unstoppable momentum of the witch-hunt, where individual betrayals lead to collective panic, which in turn provokes further betrayals. So from the opening shot (a darkness left empty by the fading of the title, into which Abigail suddenly emerges), we cut repeatedly from the private to the public, and from the cause to the consequence—from the eyes of the obsessed teenage girl to the whole gang of them dancing naked in the woods, bursting with a sexuality that Salem proves unable to contain; from Tituba, terrified and vengeful as she identifies the witches, to the orgy of false confession she elicits from the girls; from the village mob, which drags innocent women from their homes, to Proctor at work on his farm, feeding the frenzy in town by doggedly refusing to come forward with the information that could put a stop to it; from the fury of the trials to Putnam, poised to redirect that fury toward his neighbors and kill them for their land.

These juxtapositions set out to capture the visceral excitement generated by the spectacle of an entire society seized by uncontrollable madness—an excitement I felt as I read the first draft of Arthur Miller's screenplay. I made the film because I was physically seized by it—because as I turned the pages my heart beat faster, my palms sweated, and I felt in my gut the ancient stirrings of terror and pity.

Later, as we prepared to shoot the movie, we were struck time and again by its alarming topicality: it spoke directly about the bigotry of religious fundamentalists across the globe, about communities torn apart by accusations of child abuse, about the rigid intellectual orthodoxies of college campuses—there is no shortage of contemporary Salems ready to cry witchcraft. But the film's political agenda is not specific. *The Crucible* has outlived Joe McCarthy, and has acquired a universal urgency shared only by stories that tap primal truths.

It is nevertheless a story that seemed to us to require rooting in the particular circumstances that gave rise to it, and that would best achieve universal resonance in the context of its own tiny corner of the world. The creation of Salem was therefore one of our first challenges, and as we explored New England, looking for a place to build it, the landscape itself emerged for us as an integral part of the Puritan mentality. No amount of budgetary pressure to shoot the movie in Nova Scotia (where you can apparently get more for your dollar) could dislodge us from the land where the Puritans first arrived to create settlements that were to be "as a city on a hill"—an example to the rest of mankind. There is a marvelously austere beauty to northern Massachusetts that, however tough conditions may be in the winter, promises a redefinition of Eden. Like the Puritans, we had to create a community in active pursuit of perfection, which contained a reproach to the ungodly and required its inhabitants to live as saints in Paradise: a blueprint, in other words, for the small town that has become a staple of American movie iconography. Over the last hundred years, Hollywood has taken up where the Puritans left off, insisting repeatedly that the world can see an image of perfection on Main Street USA; and perhaps it is not entirely fanciful to detect the legacy of John Winthrop in the movies of Frank Capra.

A city on a hill—an image of perfection—was therefore the brief to which Andrew Dunn, my Director of Photography, and Lilly Kilvert, my Production Designer, worked. The coasts of Nova Scotia, and even Maine, were too inhospitable for us: they are hard places, which could suggest altogether the wrong explanation for the madness that engulfed Salem in 1692. The witch-hunt was not a function of the adversity of the Puritan lifestyle. On the contrary, *The Crucible* is Paradise Lost (albeit a sparse Paradise, devoid of vanity), and the presence of the Devil in Salem is a consequence of the demand to live the perfect life. So the way the film looks is more than a counterpoint to its action. The constant pressure to dedicate every aspect of life to the glory of God is what lets the Devil in, and the beauty of the surroundings is a prerequisite for the violence of what happens within them. The light gives birth to the dark.

Pioneers geographically as well as spiritually, the Puritans carved out their piece of Heaven on a narrow strip between the ocean stretching east and the boundless American wilderness stretching west. Although Salem Village, where the events of 1692 took place, was in fact a mile or so inland

(Salem Town was a harbor town, as it still is), the movie seemed to us to need constant sight of the sea, as if to accentuate the insecurity of immigrant stock. I was keen in particular to play Proctor's last scene with Elizabeth outside the jail, perched on the edge of the continent, two small figures determining between them the fate of a man's soul and the future of the whole community. (The day we shot this scene, the elements obliged us with a nor'easter as dramatically appropriate as it was brutal to work in.) In the end, we settled on Hog Island, in the mouth of the Essex River, within sight of land once owned by John Proctor. Unsurprisingly, in nearly every place on the New England coast where it might have been logical to build a town, somebody had already built one; but Hog Island is five minutes by boat from the mainland, so no one had bothered. Our pristine slice of the New World came at the cost of a flotilla of pontoon boats, which ferried us every day before dawn to work on a set largely populated, it seemed, by descendants of participants in the original witch-hunt. I would prefer to think that the conviction with which these two hundred or so locals, mostly new to acting, hurled themselves at the business of pursuing and hanging the accused was the result of my inspirational harangues; but it was hard sometimes not to suspect that it was in their Yankee blood. Mercifully, most claimed descent from the witches rather than the persecutors, Giles Corey being the ancestor of choice.

As Salem took shape, so did the shooting script. All

screenplays develop in the months of preproduction, but I still felt as if I was asking Shakespeare for amendments to *King Lear*. That we were dealing with one of the towering masterpieces of the modern theater seemed, however, only to act as a spur to its author, and I spent with him some of the most exciting days of my life, in the hut at the bottom of his Connecticut garden, *The Crucible* flashing across his computer screen as if he'd written it yesterday. The film owes everything to Arthur Miller's persistent readiness to refashion his screenplay as I strove to visualize it image by image, to feel its structures cut by cut, and to cope with the practical necessities of a fifty-six-day shoot.

The scale of the location gave us the opportunity to treat the growing panic in the village like a virus, so the first two acts of the play were substantially reworked. Abigail carries news of Betty's sickness first to the doctor and then to the Putnams; the doctor is chased away from the Parris house by villagers anxious to know what is wrong with her; the Coreys take the news to the Proctors; the entire community converges on the meeting house to hear Parris raise the possibility that the Devil might be at large; and Hale sniffs out evidence of witchcraft all over town. The steadily mounting tempo of Act One of the play is translated into a constantly shifting visual perspective and increasingly rapid cutting, which culminate back in Betty's bedroom as the delirious girls open themselves to "the light of God."

John Proctor is meanwhile in effect doing everything he

can to stay out of the movie. Elizabeth tries to push him into it, but his passivity is matched by the camera's: long, uninterrupted takes contrast with the gathering terror provoked by Danforth's arrival. Repeated cutting between the hysteria in town and the inertia at the Proctor house ultimately brings the witch-hunt to his doorstep; and when all the film's crises converge in the long court-room sequence equivalent to Act Three of the play, the camera finally stays put to observe, dispassionately, the impending catastrophe. The explosive consequences of Elizabeth Proctor's first lie cause an equivalent eruption in the camera. Swooping down on the hysterical girls as if it were the yellow bird itself, it becomes part of the contagion, and only when the village frenzy ebbs does the film recover its sobriety.

Much of the screenplay reproduces dialogue from the play more or less exactly, even if the physical context is changed. The yellow bird chases the girls out of the meeting house, down the hill and into the sea in cinematic response to the tension built up in the court; but matching the image to the word here required only minimal textual amendment to the end of the play's third act. As it happened, this sequence became one of the biggest deals of the shoot. It isn't so hard to say "I see two hundred of them, running into the water," but I guess that "Invade Normandy" also slips pretty easily off the tongue. Weeks of preparation preceded the two days over which we shot the scene—the first day shooting toward land from platforms moored a hundred yards offshore, the second shooting from the shore out to sea. Both days we had about an hour of high tide in which to get the wide shots. By the time we got to the tighter shots the tide had gone out, leaving underfoot a glutinously unphotogenic sludge, which stayed out of sight beneath the bottom of the frame. Nobody had more than one costume, so once wet they stayed wet, and we therefore had only one take to get the first frenzied dive into the sea; any take thereafter would reveal everyone to be mysteriously sodden before they hit the water. Although the wardrobe department was able to dry out the principal characters' costumes overnight, on the second day the rest of the village had to climb back into clothes still damp from the first day's operations. That they did so without a murmur of complaint was further tribute to their Puritan forebears. The girls—who got the worst of it—were elaborately underdressed in rubber diving gear: it was mid-October, and we had expected rough weather. On the day, we basked in an Indian summer that sent the temperature into the eighties, so while the crew waded around in shorts, the girls slowly baked.

Meanwhile, the sun obliged us to reexamine our lighting strategy for the long courtroom scene that culminates in the attack of the yellow bird, and which we had yet to shoot. We had planned to play it as if in the middle of a storm, reckoning that the whole event would respond well to the relentless sound of rain on the meeting house roof and to cheerlessly oppressive light seeping through the windows; and we had already shot Elizabeth Proctor's arrival at the meeting house in a downpour as heavy as our special-effects boys could muster. Now we had in the can a sequence that in real time happens only ten minutes later, and there was barely a cloud in the sky. We might have been more daunted if we had grown less accustomed to the weather in New England, where ten minutes is more than enough time for a storm to clear completely; but we still had to bring out the sun someplace between Elizabeth's arrival and the girls' hasty departure. In the event, it breaks through the clouds and floods the room just before Elizabeth denies John's adultery, surrounding her briefly in something like a halo—an effect with which we were all rather pleased, but which, like a lot of filmmaking, was as much improvisation as calculation. The best-laid plans almost invariably need relaying, and relaying again.

A different form of improvisation had been our starting point with the fifteen afflicted girls, most of them local teenagers with no professional experience, who were the first to turn up for rehearsal for a week of background exercises and movement work before the rest of the cast arrived to work on the screenplay itself. The very concept of rehearsal is treated with suspicion by much of the film world, so it was with a certain degree of skepticism that the budget was stretched to include a process that turned out to be as effective as it was unnerving. The production offices were in a deserted mental hospital, whose gymnasium provided an appropriate venue for our exploration of the outer reaches of adolescent hysteria. As it turned out, it was not too difficult to devise exercises that released the pent-up aggression of the Salem girls, and hysteria came easily. Actors rarely find much of a problem in letting rip the innate malevolence that most of us firmly suppress—it seems, in fact, to be one of the most gratifying parts of the job. So the girls were disturbingly quick to open themselves to the sensations that fueled the witch-hunt. We avoided, however, working in detail on the screenplay—everything the girls do in the film is born of panic ("What'll we do? The whole country's talkin' witchcraft!") and therefore needed an improvisatory quality, which might have been undermined by the sort of detailed textual rehearsal required in the theater to establish the foundations for a twice-nightly appearance of spontaneity. In front of the camera, there is still plenty that requires premeditation. Actors must hit their marks to stay in focus, reproduce exactly physical actions from shot to shot to preserve continuity, and, not least, remember their lines. But in the end, a scene is usually played for one day only—albeit many times over—so a more literal spontaneity is achievable; and, given the camera's brutal way of exposing anything phony, it is also desirable.

The intention, therefore, was to establish a well of shared feeling and experience from which we could draw during the shoot; and it was the first five minutes of the film that provided maybe the most interesting challenge. We worked from the premise that the source of the girls' destructive energy is their emergent sexuality, so the entire opening is designed to uncork the bottle of desire—to make flesh what in the play is past and done, referred to only. By virtue of its position at the front of the movie, the night in the forest exerts continual pressure not only on the girls, who fear exposure, but also on the apparently rigorous decorum of village life. And while it might have been obvious to open the movie with images of Puritan gravity, and to create a context for the sensual release of the séance, it seemed more dangerous to work the other way round—to taste the forbidden fruit before we enter what purports to be Eden. So, after a rapid title sequence that takes the girls out of bed and into the street, shedding cloaks and inhibitions as they crash through the forest, and pulsing with excitment as they conjure the boys they desire, we plunge straight into the dance.

But how do you dance if you have never danced before in your life? How do you release the suppressed vitality of so many years? We worked with a wonderful movement teacher from New York University on finding the most basic response to the summons of music; and as we reckoned that Tituba had brought with her from Barbados the rhythms of the Caribbean, we found an ancient voodoo fertility chant and tried to imagine how it would work on girls whose musical experience was limited to the psalm book. While this was more of a stretch than devising the courtroom hysteria, it soon became clear that the two were inseparable, and that a community that denies to its young any outlet for the expression of sexuality is asking for trouble.

For Abigail, of course, the night in the forest goes beyond the expression of sexuality—not least because with John Proctor she has already been there, and she is now bent on casting a spell to kill his wife; and while the vindictiveness of the other girls is unleashed only by the whole country talking witchcraft, Abigail—in her own mind at least—is actually practicing it. So the dance is counterpointed by close-ups of her murderously single-minded face—establishing that tension, characteristic of the whole film, between the group and the individual. However expressive the movement of the group (or, indeed, the camera) might be, it is the performance of the individual through which the film ultimately comes to life. I would have been less determined to pitch Abigail so firmly into the opening frame if I had been less confident of Winona Ryder's ability immediately to suggest the stew of conflicting emotion that propels her through the movie.

In fact, nothing about the shoot was more dependable than the quality of the acting: every actor in the English-speaking world seemed to want to be in the film, so the elaborate courtship usually required to persuade movie stars actually to take part in a movie went by the board. Daniel Day-Lewis needed no more than a cup of tea in a London café, and immediately became a close and insightful friend and collaborator. I met Winona Ryder by chance at a party, soon after the casting process began. She lamented that she wasn't five years younger; and seeing her in her party gear, I found it hard to make the connection with the Puritan teenager, so I lamented it too. But we arranged to meet for lunch a couple of days later, and I found myself sitting opposite a waif in a big white T-shirt who looked on the young side for Betty Parris. I knew Joan Allen from her work on the New York stage, which proved to be the most fertile source for our entire acting company—unsurprisingly, given the linguistic demands of the screenplay. But coming as I do from the English theater, nothing excited me more than the participation of Paul Scofield, who may be the greatest actor alive but who works nowadays only when it genuinely seems to him to be worthwhile. It would have been easy enough to find one of those actors who specialize in the sinister, but Danforth's particular danger is that his convictions are genuine and his commitment to rooting out the Devil is deeply felt. At our first meeting, Paul told me that the part kept reminding him of something else he had played, and that he had eventually realized that Danforth was in some ways the flip side of Sir Thomas More, the model of integrity at the center of *A Man for All Seasons*. Indeed, before he became a Catholic martyr at the hands of King Henry VIII, More had been an enthusiastic burner of Protestants; and one cannot help feeling that Scofield's Danforth would be as obdurate in the face of persecution as he is zealous in its application.

The first six weeks of the shoot we spent on Hog Island, thrust together each day in a community whose literal insularity fed neatly into the film. The geography of the set even dictated a shooting schedule that reflected the events we were shooting. The Proctor house, for instance, was built some distance from the village; as a result, Joan Allen was as infrequent a visitor to the main set as Elizabeth Proctor is to the village. Paul Scofield arrived halfway through the shoot, causing as much of a stir on the set as Danforth does in Salem. The entire shoot was characterized by a peculiar intensity and sense of purpose, which saw us through the three weeks we had to spend away from the island: the tavern and meeting house interiors had been constructed on a hastily improvised soundstage in a disused factory in Beverly. Here, Rob Campbell, who played Reverend Hale, watched in dismay as the witch trials were re-created in the heart of what was once Hale's own parish. We went back outdoors to shoot the jail scenes, on a stretch of the Massachusetts coast whose potential bleakness we had taken on trust when we had chosen it in the middle of the summer, and which now—gray and leaf-less—fully rewarded our confidence.

The aim always was to create the circumstances that would allow these actors fully to reveal the huge individual emotional capital invested in every twist of the communal hysteria. Proctor's guilt, Abigail's obsession with him, Parris's fear for his job, and Mary Warren's terror are as far-reaching in their effect and as thematically important as anything that happens in the trials; and ultimately, there is nothing larger in the film than the opening of the Proctors' hearts to each other. The fate of the world, of course, is bound up in Proctor's decision whether or not to make a false confession, and his defiance marks the end of the madness. But the political significance of the resolution is balanced by its unabashed emotionalism; and with Daniel Day-Lewis and Joan Allen, we were able to equate the fate of the world with the fate of a marriage.

Comparatively little was lost in postproduction. The final cut is maybe fifteen minutes shorter than the first rough cut, much of the discarded footage being gradually whittled away as I discovered with my editor, Tariq Anwar, the film's inherent rhythms. In the cutting room, as on the set, we strove for clarity and pace; and we aimed for an equivalent simplicity when we came to add the music. The score composed by George Fenton is in fact based on a fusion of different sound worlds: archaic string instruments (a viol consort), a modern symphony orchestra, synthesizers, and percussion generated by the electronic sampling of ancient ironmongery. The music, like the movie as a whole, not only speaks of the past in contemporary terms but yokes together ancient and modern to create a new world, at once strange and familiar. In *The Crucible,* an old story—much older than Salem—is played out to its inevitable completion: ever in search of the New Jerusalem, we are condemned to repeat our mistakes. But there may still be a man and a woman, alone at the edge of the world, asking each other for forgiveness.

# Contents

# A Note on the Text

This screenplay reflects the final cut of the film of *The Crucible*.

1. INT. NIGHT. BETTY PARRIS'S BEDROOM.
*A teenage girl sits up in her bed. She shakes awake the little girl who sleeps next to her. The two of them—ABIGAIL WILLIAMS and her ten-year-old cousin BETTY PARRIS—get out of bed and dress quickly.*

2. EXT. NIGHT. SALEM VILLAGE.
*ABIGAIL and BETTY surreptitiously emerge from the doorway of Parris's house, and hurry in the direction of the forest.*
*Then another cloaked figure from another house. And another.*
*They move past the last house in town and head for the forest, and now we hear hurried whispers, giggles, the voices of young girls, excited, urgent. But we can't make out what they are saying.*

3. EXT. NIGHT. FOREST.
*The fog obscures all but the great pine trunks as we catch sight of thirteen or fourteen GIRLS rushing through the forest, their excited faces intent on something ahead. Their dark capes, long skirts, and caps are snatched at by branches and thorny canes, but they crash through toward . . .*

4. EXT. NIGHT. FOREST CLEARING.
*A dozen GIRLS burst into the open. These teenagers are exploding with a primeval force toward a release, which is . . .*
*TITUBA, a Barbados slave in her thirties, crouching over a boiling kettle of water.*
*The GIRLS are round her in an instant. TITUBA motions for them to kneel round the fire.*

TITUBA: What you bring me?

*The GIRLS produce herbs, beans, etc.*

*One by one the GIRLS throw their offerings into the kettle, muttering boys' names as they do so. They are conjuring sweethearts.*

*Finally,* RUTH PUTNAM *throws a frog into the pot, and* ABIGAIL *gives the rooster she has been carrying to* TITUBA.

TITUBA *suddenly waves the rooster over the group, and with a scream they scatter, laughing.* TITUBA *starts to chant, waving the rooster to and fro. The GIRLS take up the rhythm, and an impromptu dance begins. Their movements become more and more free and joyful, and an inspired* MERCY LEWIS *calls to* TITUBA—

MERCY LEWIS: Make a spell on Joseph Baker, Tituba! Make him love me!

*Whoops of thrilled voices, and all the GIRLS call out the names of the boys they desire.*

*All but four of the GIRLS are approaching a joyful hysteria.*

*But* BETTY PARRIS *and* RUTH PUTNAM *watch in wide-eyed terror, and* MARY WARREN *takes no part—she is the scared and tempted observer.*

*And* ABIGAIL *crouches by the kettle, staring blankly at* TITUBA *with the rooster, intent on some private desire of her own. One of the GIRLS spots her and goes close to her.*

JOANNA PRESTON: Abby!—Who do you want!

HANNAH BROWN: She wants John Proctor!

*At this, a screaming uproar.* ABIGAIL *remains intent on the chanting* TITUBA.

JOANNA PRESTON: Get her John Proctor again, Tituba!

ABIGAIL *ignores* JOANNA *and then goes close to* TITUBA. *The rhythms are wild now, as she whispers avidly into* TITUBA's *ear . . .*

TITUBA: No—Abby, that be a bad t'ing!

ABIGAIL *defiantly grabs the rooster from* TITUBA *and violently thrashes it against the kettle, catching the blood in her palm and raising it to her lips.*

TITUBA: Abby—no!

*Defying* TITUBA, ABIGAIL *drinks from her palm. A climactic scream of release from all around—as* MERCY LEWIS *and several others tear off their clothes and dance naked.*

5. EXT. NIGHT. FOREST.
REVEREND PARRIS *hurrying through the woods, listening for the now-nearby sounds of girls. A look on his face of incredulousness and alarm as he presses ahead.*

6. EXT. NIGHT. FOREST CLEARING.
PARRIS *sees the clearing ahead through the trees, his face absolutely horrified at the sight of* TWO GIRLS, *who, having spotted him, rush away; they are naked, clutching their clothing.* MERCY LEWIS, *naked, is sprinting toward the trees.*

GIRLS: It's the minister! [Etc.]

TITUBA *has managed to dive out of sight and escape.*
BETTY PARRIS *is screaming in terror as* ABIGAIL
*tries to drag her away unsuccessfully.*

ABIGAIL: Come away! He'll see us!

BETTY: I can't move! Help me! No! [Etc.]


7. EXT. NIGHT. FOREST CLEARING.
PARRIS *is horrified as he investigates the debris of the kettle—
the herbs, the frog, the rooster—and then he faces his niece* ABI-
GAIL *and his screaming daughter,* BETTY.


8. INT. DAY. BETTY PARRIS'S BEDROOM.
*The following morning.* BETTY *is asleep.* ABIGAIL *turns in
fear as* PARRIS *enters, carrying a birch rod.* TITUBA *is col-
lecting food for breakfast.* PARRIS *ignores her.*

PARRIS: Dress the child and come to my study.

 ABIGAIL *pulls* BETTY*'s arms to raise her; as* PARRIS
 *turns, he sees* BETTY *fall back unconscious to the pillow.*

ABIGAIL: Betty. Betty?

 *But* BETTY *lies inert.* PARRIS *returns to the room,
 instantly alarmed.*

PARRIS: Betty!

 BETTY *doesn't move.*


9. EXT. DAY. SALEM VILLAGE.
ABIGAIL *exits Parris's house and hurries through the village. A
couple of* LOUTS *hauling hay give her a knowing eye as she
passes, and she angrily turns away and hurries to . . .*

## 10. EXT. DAY. DOCTOR GRIGGS'S HOUSE.

*The front door is opening;* MRS. GRIGGS *stands there.*

ABIGAIL: If it please, Mrs. Griggs, Reverend Parris asks for the doctor to come at once. Betty is gone sick—she can't wake.

MRS. GRIGGS: *(Big surprise)* Can't she!—the doctor's gone to the Putnams'—their Ruth can't wake either. *This news is an alarming clap for* ABIGAIL; *she rushes off, leaving an extremely curious* MRS. GRIGGS *staring after her.*


## 11. INT. DAY. RUTH PUTNAM'S BEDROOM.

DR. GRIGGS *has just examined* RUTH. PARRIS *has arrived with* ABIGAIL *and waits, with* THOMAS *and* ANN PUTNAM *and* MERCY LEWIS, *the doctor's verdict.*

GRIGGS: I fear there be no medicines for this; I have seen nothing like it before. There be no fever nor wound . . . and yet she sleeps.

PARRIS: Oh dear Lord, my Betty is the same!
*All eyes swerve to* PARRIS; *the* PUTNAMS *are especially fired up, and for different reasons* ABIGAIL *and* MERCY. PARRIS *suddenly notices that* RUTH's *eyes are wide open.*

PUTNAM: The same?

PARRIS: . . . only *her* eyes are closed.

ANN PUTNAM: It's the Devil, isn't it; the Devil is taking hold of them.

GRIGGS: Oh, Goody Putnam, I know not . . .

ANN PUTNAM: Doctor, I beg you . . . she is my last, my only! I cannot lose her!

GRIGGS: I shall do all I can, Goody Putnam—but this may be a sickness beyond my art . . .

ANN PUTNAM: (Screaming at PUTNAM) Thomas!

12. EXT. DAY. PUTNAM'S HOUSE.

GRIGGS, PARRIS, and ABIGAIL are leaving.

PARRIS: I beg you, we cannot leap to witchcraft for the cause of this.

PUTNAM: Don't you understand it, sir? There are hurtful vengeful spirits laying hand on these children. Let you take hold here. Let no one charge you. Declare it yourself.

PARRIS: Not yet! I need time; I must think, I must pray.

GRIGGS: Yes, I agree with Reverend Parris—good day to you, sir.

PUTNAM angrily watches them depart.

13. EXT. DAY. PARRIS'S HOUSE.

GRIGGS emerges from the house and pushes his way through agitated townsfolk, including HERRICK.

HERRICK: She still sleeps then, Doctor?

GRIGGS tries to brush him off.

MAN: She flies, y'know.

GRIGGS: Flies! Oh come now, man.

HERRICK: George Collins seen her with his own eyes.

GRIGGS: Seen what?

HERRICK: The minister's daughter goin' over Ingersoll's barn.

MAN: . . . And comes down light as a bird!

*ABIGAIL has been watching all this from BETTY's window.*

14. INT. DAY. BETTY PARRIS'S BEDROOM.

*PARRIS watches over BETTY still asleep in bed. ABIGAIL turns from the window.*

ABIGAIL: Uncle? Perhaps you ought to go down and tell the people . . .

PARRIS: And what shall I tell them! That my daughter and my niece I discovered dancing like heathen in the forest?

ABIGAIL: We did dance, and let me be whipped if I must be—but they're talking of witchcraft—Betty's not witched.

PARRIS: Were you conjuring spirits in the forest? I want the truth now.

ABIGAIL: We never conjured spirits.

PARRIS: Now hear me, child. You must know that there is a faction in the church sworn to drive me from my pulpit . . .

ABIGAIL: Oh, I know that, sir.

PARRIS: And they will destroy me now if my own house turns out to be the center of some obscene practice! Now I saw someone naked running through the trees.

ABIGAIL: No one was . . .

PARRIS: *(Smashing her across the cheek)* Don't lie to me, I saw it!

ABIGAIL: . . . It were only sport, Uncle!

PARRIS: *(Pointing down at BETTY)* You call this sport!— She cannot wake! *(ABIGAIL clamps shut; he shifts his tack.)* Now give me upright answer—your name in the town . . . is entirely white, is it not?

ABIGAIL: There be no blush about my name, sir!

PARRIS: *(Taking courage in hand)* Why did Goody Proctor discharge you from her service?

ABIGAIL: *(In full confrontation—wild)* Because I refused to be her slave!

PARRIS: *(With difficulty)* I have heard said that John Proctor . . . John Proctor and you . . .

ABIGAIL: My name is good in the village—Elizabeth Proctor is an envious, gossiping liar!

*The hubbub outside increases. TITUBA appears in the stairway.*

TITUBA: Mr. Parris, them asking for you. You must come down, sir.

*PARRIS leaves hurriedly. TITUBA rushes to BETTY's side to comfort her.*

TITUBA: Betty, my sweet, wake up. Wake up, Betty.

ABIGAIL: *(Shoving TITUBA out of the way)* Betty . . . stop this now!! I know you hear me . . . Wake up, now!! *(Yells into her face)* Betty!

*In open fear for herself she releases BETTY, who falls back, limp.* PARRIS *is heard offscreen trying to calm the curious and frightened townsfolk.*

## 15. Ext. Day. Field on Proctor's Farm.

JOHN PROCTOR *is scything wheat. His two SONS are working nearby.*

ELIZABETH, *his wife, is approaching across the field; from twenty yards off she indicates their house and calls.*

ELIZABETH: John! Giles and Martha are here!

    *He starts toward her.*

## 16. Ext. Day. Proctor's House.

PROCTOR *and* ELIZABETH *are approaching* GILES *and* MARTHA COREY. *He is turning eighty; his wife,* MAR-THA, *is in her forties. She flaunts a red sash around her waist.*

MARY WARREN, *the* PROCTORS' *servant, tends to the* COREYS' *gig.*

COREY: You've got to come with me to the village, John. Mr. Parris—God help us—has summoned a meeting of the society.

ELIZABETH: What for?

MARTHA: What for! When did that man ever call a meeting except for his own benefit.

COREY: I'm explaining it, Martha.

MARTHA: I'm sorry not to have noticed.

    *The* PROCTORS *exchange knowing glances, suppressing grins.*

MARTHA: They're saying his daughter Betty's been witched.

PROCTOR: Witched!

COREY: Aye, she sleeps and can't be waked . . . and the Putnam girl, too, they say.

MARTHA: What do you know of this silliness, Mary Warren?

MARY WARREN: Nothing!

*The COREYS mount their gig.*

COREY: I smell mischief here. You must come with me, John; the folk will be looking to your judgment.

ELIZABETH: *(To PROCTOR)* How can they not wake up?

PROCTOR: God knows . . . You go right ahead, Giles. I'll be along.

*The COREYS leave, and the PROCTORS slowly go into the house.*


17. INT. DAY. PROCTOR'S COMMON ROOM.

PROCTOR *is getting into a coat.* ELIZABETH *works by the fire.*

PROCTOR: *(As he makes to leave)* There are still flowers in the fields; you might cut some. It's winter in here yet.

ELIZABETH: *(Blaming herself and resisting it)* Aye! I'll cut some flowers.

*He exits into the yard. We stay with her as she watches him go—anxiety on her face, a desire to express and an inability.*

18. Ext. Day. Meeting House.

*The* VILLAGERS *pour into the meeting house.*

*At the busy front door to the meeting house,* GOODY OS-
BURN *and* GOODY GOOD *are begging.*

GOODY OSBURN: Give a penny! Give a penny, annoy
    the Devil!

PUTNAM: *(Pushing her aside)* Goody Osburn, you have no
    permission to beg here!

    *Surrounded by horses, gigs, and carts,* GILES *helps* MAR-
    THA *down from their gig.* MARTHA *halts, chilled by
    some hostile sense.*

MARTHA: I'll wait for you . . . I fear this.

COREY: Fear it! Why?

    *But she starts away, against the crowd. He continues inside.*


19. Int. Day. Meeting House.

PARRIS *is seated beside the pulpit. The meeting house is
packed. At the back sit the* GIRLS, *not all in a row but scattered
near one another.*

PARRIS *leaves his chair and steps to the pulpit.*

PARRIS: Let us quiet our hearts! *(The* CONGREGA-
    TION *grows silent.)* You are all aware of the rumors
    . . . of that spirit come among us out of Hell; that
    hateful enemy of God and all Christian people—the
    Devil. Now, I have invited Reverend John Hale of
    Beverly to come to Salem.

    *The* CONGREGATION *stirs with intense interest.*

PARRIS: *(Continuing)* He has delved deeply into all demonic arts, and will surely go to the bottom of this. You may recall that in Beverly last year they believed they had a witch, until Mister Hale examined her and decided she was innocent to witchcraft . . .

*PARRIS's eye catches an indignant PUTNAM's, so he changes his tack.*

PARRIS: *(Continuing)* . . . But it may well be that in Salem he will find the signs of Lucifer, and if so, you may be sure, he will hunt him down! Let us turn our hearts to Psalm Seventy-three, "Sure God is good to Israel."

*As the CONGREGATION starts to sing, the GIRLS look in excited fear to ABIGAIL, who immediately makes herself small and heads silently for the door. The OTH-ERS follow.*


20. EXT. DAY. SALEM VILLAGE.
*The GIRLS move hurriedly to PARRIS's house.*


21. INT. DAY. BETTY PARRIS'S BEDROOM.
*The psalm can be heard as ABIGAIL storms into the room, followed by MERCY LEWIS and the rest. She strides directly to BETTY and sits poised over her.*

ABIGAIL: You will stop this now! *(Yells into her face)* Betty!

*MERCY leans in and smashes BETTY across the face.*
*MARY WARREN rushes in. She is a meager girl, near terror now.*

MARY WARREN: What'll we do! The whole country's talkin' witchcraft!

MERCY LEWIS: She means to tell!

MARY WARREN: We've got to tell or they'll be callin' us witches! Witchery's a hangin' error, like they done in Boston two year ago! You'll only be whipped for trying to conjure the boys and the dancing!

*ABIGAIL and MERCY, taking this to heart, turn back to BETTY. MERCY makes a move to beat her again, but ABIGAIL stops her.*

ABIGAIL: Now listen to me, Betty dear—I talked to your Papa, and I told him everything, so there's nothing to be feared anymore.

*BETTY opens her eyes, startling ABIGAIL and the other GIRLS.*

BETTY: I want my Mama!

ABIGAIL: Your Mama's dead and buried!

BETTY: I'll fly to her! Let me fly!

*Arms raised, she springs to the window. ABIGAIL and MERCY struggle to hold her back.*

ABIGAIL: Why are you doing this? I've told him. He knows now.

BETTY: You drank blood, Abby, you didn't tell him that!

*ABIGAIL smashes BETTY across the face.*

ABIGAIL: You never say that again!

BETTY: You drank a charm to kill John Proctor's wife!

MERCY LEWIS: No, Abby.

BETTY: You drank a charm to kill Goody Proctor!

ABIGAIL: Shut it!

> ABIGAIL *grabs her from* MERCY *and throws her on the bed with a smash to the face. The* GIRLS *run to the stairs, all crying with fear.*

MARY WARREN: Abby, she's going to die!

ABIGAIL: Now look you, all of you!—We danced. And that is all. And mark this—let anyone breathe a word or the edge of a word about the other things, and I will come to you in the black of some terrible night and I will bring with me a pointy reckoning that will shudder you. And you know I can do it; I saw Indians smash my dear parents' heads on the pillow next to mine, and I have seen some reddish work done at night—and I can make you wish you'd never seen the sun go down!

> *In a flash and with a terrible scream,* BETTY *in panic is across the room and is almost out the window—the* GIRLS *scream as* ABIGAIL *and a few* OTHERS *rush to grab her.*

## 22. INT. DAY. MEETING HOUSE.

BETTY's *screams cut through the singing. The* CONGREGATION *starts to stream out.*

## 23. EXT. DAY. PARRIS'S HOUSE.

*The* CONGREGATION *looks up in amazement at* BETTY, *hanging out of the window. As the* CONGREGATION *calls* out to her, *the* PUTNAMS, PARRIS, *and* OTHERS *run into Parris's house.*

## 24. INT. DAY. BETTY PARRIS'S BEDROOM.

*At the window,* ABIGAIL, MERCY, *and* ANOTHER *pull* BETTY *back into the room and throw her onto the bed.*

BETTY: Mama! Mama!

MERCY LEWIS: Keep still, little devil!

PARRIS: Betty! Oh, Betty! Oh, dear God.

MERCY LEWIS: It's when she heard the psalm, I think —she run straight for the window.

ANN PUTNAM: Mark it for a sign, Mr. Parris! My mother told me that!

> GILES COREY *is meanwhile helping the community's senior member,* REBECCA NURSE, *up the stairs.*

REBECCA: *(To* COREY*)* There is hard sickness here, Giles Corey, so please to keep the quiet.

COREY: I've not said a word, nobody can testify I've said a word!

> *On their entry an explosion of whimpering from* BETTY.

PARRIS: Rebecca, I fear we are lost.

ANN PUTNAM: She cannot bear to hear the Lord's name—that's a notorious sign of witchcraft afoot, Rebecca!

> REBECCA *goes to the bedside, feels* BETTY*'s forehead.*
> ABIGAIL *goes to shut the window and sees, in the open*

*area behind the meeting house,* PROCTOR *tying his horse to a railing and talking to* CHEEVER.

BETTY *has subsided under* REBECCA's *hand and seems to sleep peacefully.*

ANN PUTNAM: *(Mysteriously)* What have you done?

PUTNAM: Goody Nurse, will you go to our Ruth and see if you can wake her?

REBECCA: I think she'll wake when she tires of it. I am twenty-six times a grandma; they can run you bow-legged in their silly seasons.


25. INT. DAY. PARLOR OF PARRIS'S HOUSE.

REBECCA is leading them ALL *downstairs, where* PROC-TOR is waiting for them.

REBECCA: —So you've sent for Reverend Hale of Beverly, Mr. Parris.

PARRIS: Only to satisfy all that the Devil is not among us. *(Noticing* PROCTOR*)* Mr. Proctor.

REBECCA: Ah, John, come help us. We are all at sea.

PROCTOR: Why did you not call for a meeting before you decided to look for devils?

PUTNAM: A man cannot pick his teeth without some sort of meeting in this society—I'm sick of meetings!

PROCTOR: The society will not be a bag to swing around your head, Mr. Putnam!

PARRIS *and* PUTNAM *shout back at him.*

REBECCA: Peace. Peace, dear friends!

*As* ABIGAIL *comes in,* PROCTOR *can't help catch her with his glance.*

REBECCA: Mr. Parris, I think you'd best send Reverend Hale back as soon as he come. This will set us all to arguing again in the society. Let us rather blame ourselves than the Devil . . .

PUTNAM: Blame ourselves! How can we blame ourselves! I'm one of nine sons—the Putnam seed have peopled this province . . .

ANN PUTNAM: . . . And we have but one child left of eight.

REBECCA: Goody Ann, we can only go to God for the cause of that.

ANN PUTNAM: God! You think it be God's work that you have never lost a child or grandchild either, and I bury all but one?

PROCTOR: And who or what give us leave to decide what is God's work, Goody Putnam, and what is not. God never spoke in my ear and I can't think of anyone else he's done the favor! Your pardon, Rebecca. *He leaves.*


26. EXT. DAY. BEHIND THE MEETING HOUSE.

PROCTOR *is about to untie his horse when* ABIGAIL *appears. She advances cautiously, nervously. He approaches her.*

PROCTOR: *(Grinning at her deviltry)* Is this your mischief—huh? I hear the child goes flying through the air.

ABIGAIL: Oh, she never flew—we were dancin' in the woods; my uncle leaped in on us. She took fright, is all.

PROCTOR: *(Laughs)* You'll be clapped in the stocks before you're twenty.

ABIGAIL: Oh, John, give me a soft word.

PROCTOR: No, Abby, that's done with.

ABIGAIL: . . . I am waitin' for you every night.

PROCTOR: You cannot—I never gave you hope to wait for me.

ABIGAIL: I have something better than hope, I think!

PROCTOR: Child . . .

ABIGAIL: How do you call me child!

PROCTOR: Wipe it out of mind—you must. I'll not be coming for you more.

ABIGAIL: You're surely sportin' with me.

PROCTOR: You know me better.

ABIGAIL: I know how you sweated like a stallion whenever I come near you. I saw your face when she put me out; you loved me then and you do now!

PROCTOR: Abby, I may think of you softly from time to time, but I will cut off my hand before I reach for you again. We never touched.

ABIGAIL: Aye, but we did.

*She pulls his face to her and kisses him; he presses her away violently and walks toward his horse.*

ABIGAIL: Oh, I marvel how a strong man may let such a sickly wife be . . .

PROCTOR: You'll speak nothing of Elizabeth!

ABIGAIL: She is blackening my name in the village, telling lies about me! She's a cold sniveling woman and you bend to her!

PROCTOR: Do you look for whipping?

ABIGAIL: I look for John Proctor who put knowledge in my heart! I never knew what pretense Salem was— these Christian women and their covenanted men, and all of them boiling in lust! And now you bid me go dead to all you taught me? *I know you, John Proctor!*—you loved me, and whatever sin it is, you love me yet!

*She strides away toward Parris's house.* PROCTOR'*s eye follows her and he sees . . .*

### 27. Ext. Day. Parris's House.

HALE'*s horse and gig enters the village, followed by curious townsfolk.*

PROCTOR *goes to* HALE, *who has parked by the Parris house.* HALE *is unloading enormous tomes.*

PROCTOR: *(To* HALE*)* Can I help you?

HALE: Why, thank you.

HALE *hands* PROCTOR *a couple of the heavy books.*

PROCTOR: Heavy books!

HALE: Well they must be, they are weighted with authority.

PROCTOR: I am John Proctor, Mr. Hale.

HALE: You have afflicted children?

PROCTOR: My children are as healthy as bull calves, sir—like all the other children in this village. There are wheels within wheels here, Mr. Hale, I hope you'll not forget that . . .

*As they approach the house, they see the following furious argument through the windows (which overlaps their dialogue).*


28. INT./EXT. DAY. PARRIS'S PARLOR.

PARRIS: And where is my wood! My contract provides I be supplied with all of my firewood . . .

COREY: . . . You are allowed six pound a year to buy your wood . . .

PARRIS: That six pound is part of my salary, Mr. Corey!

COREY: Salary sixty pound, plus six pound for firewood!

PARRIS: I am not some preaching farmer with a book under my arm, I am a graduate of Harvard College!

COREY: Aye, and well instructed in arithmetic!

*PROCTOR and HALE watch and listen from the threshold.*

PARRIS: I cannot fathom you people!—I can never offer one proposition but I face a howling riot of argument! I have often wondered if the Devil be in it somewhere!

PROCTOR: *(To HALE, aside)* Welcome to Salem.

*PARRIS suddenly sees HALE and approaches him, along with the PUTNAMS.*

PARRIS: Mr. Hale! How good to see you! I see you've come well prepared. This is Thomas Putnam.

PUTNAM: *(Rushing to take the books from* HALE*)* How do you do, sir? Allow me, sir! This is my wife, Goody Ann.

ANN PUTNAM: Will you come to our Ruth? Her soul seems flown away. Will you come to her?

HALE: Aye, I'll come directly. *(Turns to* REBECCA *and* NURSE*)* You must be Rebecca Nurse. And Mr. Nurse.

REBECCA: You know me?

HALE: No, but you look as such a good soul should—all of us in Beverly have heard of your great charities.

REBECCA: There is prodigious danger in seeking loose spirits; I fear it. Francis.

NURSE: *(Taking* REBECCA*'s arm)* Mr. Hale.

REBECCA: I go to God for you, sir.

PARRIS: I hope you do not mean that we go to Satan here!

REBECCA: I wish I knew.

*The* NURSES *leave.*

PROCTOR: I hear you be a sensible man, Mr. Hale—I hope you'll leave some of it in Salem.

*PROCTOR leaves.*


29. INT. DAY. BETTY PARRIS'S BEDROOM.

*They are gathered around the bed.* HALE *sits by* BETTY *and turns her hand, examines the palm and between the fingers. He bends her ear, looking behind it, then the other—he rubs her eyebrows and smells his own fingers after doing so. He goes to his book, turning a page.*

ANN PUTNAM: Our child cannot wake, sir, she lies as though dead.

PUTNAM: And this one cannot bear the Lord's name—that's a sure sign of witchcraft afloat.

HALE: No, no, Mr. Putnam, we cannot look to superstition in this. The marks of the Devil are as definite as stone.

PARRIS: What book is that?

ANN PUTNAM: What's there, sir?

HALE: Here is all the invisible world; in these books the Devil stands stripped of all his brute disguises. Here are all your familiar spirits: your incubi, and succubi, your witches that go by land, by air, and by sea. Have no fear now—we shall find him out if he has come among us, and I mean to crush him utterly if he has shown his face!

ABIGAIL *slips into the room.*

PARRIS: Here is my niece, Abigail.

HALE *barely acknowledges her. He turns to* PUTNAM.

HALE: I would like to examine your Ruth before I say more.

30. EXT. DAY. ROAD.
*The* PUTNAMS *are leading* HALE *and a small* CROWD *of fascinated onlookers toward their house.*

COREY: *(Barging in)* Mr. Hale—I've always wanted to ask a learned man—what signifies the readin' of strange books? Many a night I've waked and found her in a corner, readin' of a book, and not the Bible either . . .

HALE: Who's that?

COREY: Martha, my wife. I'm not sayin' the Devil's touched her, but mark this . . . last night I tried and tried and could not say my prayers; then she close her book and walked out of the house—and suddenly— mark this—I could pray again!

HALE: The stoppage of prayer . . . we'll discuss that.

> The PUTNAMS, HALE, PARRIS, *and* ABIGAIL *proceed toward the house, leaving* COREY *behind.*

## 31. INT. DAY. RUTH PUTNAM'S BEDROOM.

*As the* OTHERS *watch,* HALE *paces the room trying to work it all out.*

HALE: Was there no warning of this affliction? Do you recall any sort of . . . disturbance, perhaps . . . any unusual behavior?

PARRIS: *(Sighing nervously, gathering his wits)* Mr. Hale.

HALE: Mr. Parris?

PARRIS: . . . I did discover my niece . . . with a number of her friends—dancing in the forest.

HALE: *(Shocked)* You permit dancing?

PARRIS: No, no!—It were secret.

ANN PUTNAM: *(Unable to hold back)* Mr. Parris's slave has knowledge of conjurin', sir.

PARRIS: That may not be true!

HALE: Abigail . . . you must tell me about this dancing . . .

MERCY LEWIS: *(Instantly breaking in)* Common dancing is all it is, sir.

HALE: Tell me, child . . . when you are dancing, is there a fire?

ABIGAIL: Why . . .

PARRIS: There was a fire—they were boiling something . . .

ABIGAIL: Lentils and beans!

HALE: *(To PARRIS)* Was anything moving in the pot?

ABIGAIL: That jumped in, we never put that in!

HALE: What jumped in?

ABIGAIL *and* MERCY *stare silently at the floor.* HALE *senses meat.*

HALE: *(To PARRIS)* I must see these other girls! *(To ABIGAIL)* Who are they? I want their names.


32. INT. LATE AFTERNOON. MEETING HOUSE.

*The* GIRLS *are seated in a row facing* HALE *in the meeting house.* PARRIS *is with the* PUTNAMS.

HALE: Someone called the Devil in that forest! Who was it led you to dance around the fire? You can save yourselves if you tell me who it was. Was there one among you who drank from the kettle? Was there perhaps a casting of spells? Was there!

MARY WARREN *starts raising her pointing finger toward* ABIGAIL.

ABIGAIL: Not I! It wasn't me. I swear it!

HALE: These two children may be dying! Who?

ABIGAIL: Tituba!

ANN PUTNAM: *(Explodes)* I knew it!

33. EXT. LATE AFTERNOON. TITUBA'S CABIN.

*They are pulling* TITUBA *from her hut.*

PARRIS: Tituba!

PUTNAM: Come out here, now!

ABIGAIL: She made me do it! She made Betty do it!

TITUBA: Tituba no do bad t'ing . . .

*They throw* TITUBA *to the ground.*

ABIGAIL: She made me drink blood!

HALE: You drank *blood?*

ANN PUTNAM: My babies' blood? Who murdered my babies, Tituba?

*Dumbstruck,* TITUBA *is silent.*

ANN PUTNAM: I want their names! Who are they!

*All his frustration in his raised arm,* PARRIS *stands over* TITUBA, *ready to strike with a rod.*

HALE: Why can the girls not wake? Did you send your spirit out to silence them?

TITUBA: I love me Betty!

PUTNAM: Let's hang her! Hang the bitch!

TITUBA: No, no, don't hang Tituba!

HALE: You conjured her to be silent, have you not?

TITUBA: *(Points to* ABIGAIL*) She* beg me conjure, *she* beg me make charm!

ABIGAIL: She lies! She sends her spirit into me in church; she makes me laugh at prayer.

PARRIS: She have often laughed at prayer!

ABIGAIL: She comes into me when I sleep, she makes me dream corruptions!

TITUBA: Why you say bad t'ing, Abby!

ABIGAIL: Some nights I wake and I find myself standing naked in the open doorway, without a stitch on my body! . . . And she makes me do that, singing her damned Barbados songs, tempting me!

HALE: *(Certain now, resolved)* Tituba, when did you compact with the Devil? Tell me!

TITUBA: I don't, I don't compact with the Devil!

PARRIS *smashes the whip down on her repeatedly.*

PARRIS: Confess yourself or I will beat you to your death!

TITUBA: No! No!

TITUBA *sees she is facing her end. She pleads desperately.*

TITUBA: No—no! I . . . I tell him . . . I tell him I don't desire . . . I don't desire to work for him.

*A silence; she looks from insane face to insane face.*

HALE: Then you saw him?—You poor woman, he has you by the throat this very moment, doesn't he?

TITUBA, *longing for this softening in* HALE, *can only,*

*in effect, submissively agree.* HALE *suddenly takes her hand.*

## 34. INT. DUSK. BETTY PARRIS'S BEDROOM.

*They gather around the bed where* BETTY *lies inert. The* GIRLS' *tensions are very high—they don't know where this cat is going to land.*

HALE: Now, Tituba, I am going to break his grip on both of you; I am going to pry open the hands of Lucifer. *(He gently lifts her face.)* You would be a good Christian woman once again, would you not?

TITUBA: Aye, sir, a good Christian woman . . .

HALE: You do still love God?

TITUBA: I love Him with all my bein'.

HALE: *(Takes her hands in communion)* Now in God's holy name . . .

TITUBA: Oh bless Him, bless Him . . .

HALE: And to his glory . . .

TITUBA: Oh eternal gloree . . . my sweet dear Jesus . . .

HALE: Open yourself, receive his cleansing light within you! Do you want that light?

TITUBA: Oh, I want that light! Save me, Mr. Hale!

HALE: I will—if you open your heart to me. Now when the Devil comes to you, does he bring other people?

ANN PUTNAM: Sarah Good? Does he bring Goody Good?

PARRIS: Are they men or women?

TITUBA: Oh, I couldn't see, it was black dark . . .

PARRIS: You could see him, why couldn't you see others?

TITUBA: (Cornered, desperate) They was always talking, runnin' around, carryin' on so!

PARRIS: You mean out of Salem! Salem witches?

TITUBA: Why I believe so; yes, sir.

HALE: —I will protect you; you know the Devil can never overcome a minister, do you not?

TITUBA: Oh I know that, sir.

HALE: Tituba—God put you in our hands to help cleanse this village; you are God's eyes! Now face God and speak utterly—who came to you with the Devil? Two? Three? Four?

TITUBA *looks up at their blazing eyes.*

ANN PUTNAM: Was Sarah Good with him, or Osburn?

PARRIS: Their names, their names!

*His face so close to hers floods her with a sudden hatred, which her new power paradoxically releases.*

TITUBA: (Trembling with anger) How many time he bid me kill you, Mr. Parris!

PARRIS: Kill me!

TITUBA: "Rise up, Tituba, and cut that man throat!"—that's what 'im tell me. I say, "No, Devil, I don't hate that man." Him say, "Tituba, you work for me, I make you free; I give you pretty dress to wear, I put you way high up in the air, and you goin' fly back home to Barbados!" And I say, "No, Devil, you lie!" And then him come to me one stormy night and him say, "Tituba, look! I has *white* people belong to me!"

*They are hanging on her every word, and* TITUBA *has the feel of a power she never has known in her life.*

TITUBA: And I look! I look—and there was Sarah Good.

ANN PUTNAM: I knew it!—Oh bless you, Tituba!

TITUBA: *(Accepted at last!)* Aye—and Goody Osburn!

ANN PUTNAM: *(To* HALE*)* I knew it! They were mid-wives to me three times, and my babies shriveled in their hands!

ABIGAIL: I want to open myself!

*All turn to her, startled.*

ABIGAIL: I want the light of God, I want the sweet love of Jesus!

*In the throes, with* MERCY *looking up at her, enthralled and inspired too. Here at last is acceptance and holiness— and somehow vengeance.*

ABIGAIL: I did dance for the Devil! I saw him; I wrote in his book; I go back to Jesus, I kiss His hand! *(Riding her feeling)* I saw Sarah Good with the Devil! I saw Goody Osburn with the Devil!

MERCY LEWIS: I saw Bridget Bishop with the Devil!

*Now* BETTY *sits up.*

BETTY: I saw Goody Howe with the Devil! I saw Goody Barrow with the Devil!

PARRIS: She speaks, she speaks!

*Chaos. The* GIRLS *are screaming names.*

HALE: Hallelujah! Glory be to God, it is broken—they
    are free!

> *They rush out of the room.*

PUTNAM: Where's the marshal? Arrest Sarah Osburn!


## 35. Ext. Day. Edge of Proctor's Farm.

*PROCTOR and COREY are walking toward the house in
the middle distance. They see a MAN riding away from the
house, and ELIZABETH standing there watching him depart.*

COREY: *(O.S.)* Sarah Good in the jail—would you be-
    lieve a court would ever bother to jail that silly old
    turtle.

ELIZABETH: *(Calling from the house)* John. Giles. News
    from the village—there were six more accused today.

PROCTOR: More mischief here, Giles.

ELIZABETH: The town's gone wild, I think.


## 36. Ext. Day. Proctor's House/Farm.

*PROCTOR and COREY approach ELIZABETH.*

ELIZABETH: And now they've sent to Boston for the
    Deputy Governor to take charge.

COREY: Oh that's Danforth—he'll bring some sense to
    it. That's good news.

ELIZABETH: Judge Hathorne has condemned fourteen
    more people to the jail last night.

PROCTOR: Fourteen!

ELIZABETH: And promise hangin' if they don't confess.

PROCTOR: Confess? To what?

ELIZABETH: Bewitchin' the children—Abigail Williams suffers most of all, he says.

*A certain look passes between* PROCTOR *and* ELIZA-BETH—*guilt in his eyes and in hers a plea for action from him.*

COREY: *(Shaken by this news)* Save my cider. I'll go home now, tell Martha.


37. INT. DAY. PROCTOR'S COMMON ROOM.

PROCTOR *and* ELIZABETH *eat in uncomfortable silence. Finally* ELIZABETH *rises and begins to clear the table.*

PROCTOR: I am thinking if the crop comes good I'll buy George Jacobs' heifer. How would that please you?

ELIZABETH: Aye, it would.

PROCTOR: I mean to please you, Elizabeth.

*She nods; she forces herself to speak as pleasantly as she can.*

ELIZABETH: It would be well if you went to Salem. *(Pause)* Abigail told you it had naught to do with witchcraft, did she not? They say Ezekiel Cheever is clerk of the court now—can you not tell him? *(Pause)* God forbid you keep that from the court, John.

PROCTOR: It's a wonder they do believe her.

ELIZABETH: But they do! Mary Warren says that where Abigail walks the crowds part like the sea for Israel. *(Slight pause)* I think you must go at once. *(Slight pause)* I would go tonight, John. Will you?

PROCTOR: I will think on it.

ELIZABETH: You cannot keep it, John.

PROCTOR: I say I will think on it.

*Rebuffed, she starts to wash the dirty dishes in silence.*

PROCTOR: How will I prove what she told me, Elizabeth? We were alone together; I have no proof of what she said.

ELIZABETH: *(Approaching him apprehensively)* . . . You were alone with her?

PROCTOR: . . . For a moment alone, aye.

ELIZABETH: Then it is not as you told me.

PROCTOR: For a moment is all—there were others close by . . .

ELIZABETH: Do as you wish, then.

PROCTOR: Woman.

*She turns.*

PROCTOR: I'll not have your suspicion anymore.

ELIZABETH: Now John, if it were not Abigail that you must go to hurt, would you falter now? I think not.

PROCTOR: You will not judge me more, Elizabeth! I have forgot Abigail, and . . .

ELIZABETH: And I.

PROCTOR: Spare me! You forget nothing and forgive nothing. In this seven month since she is gone I have not moved from there to there without I think to please you, but an everlasting funeral still marches round your heart.

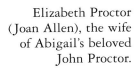

Tituba (Charlayne Woodard) casts spells to find sweethearts for the Salem girls.

Abigail (Winona Ryder) conjures the Devil to kill a rival.

Elizabeth Proctor (Joan Allen), the wife of Abigail's beloved John Proctor.

Thomas Putnam (Jeffrey Jones) rages at Tituba, believing she has bewitched his child. Rumors of witchcraft infect the village.

Playwright Arthur Miller talks with Winona Ryder.

John Proctor (Daniel Day-Lewis) rejects Abigail's advances and demands she end her accusations of witchcraft.

Judge Danforth (Paul Scofield) and Reverend Parris (Bruce Davison) struggle with Mary Warren (Karron Graves), who is terrified by Abigail's demonic visions.

The judges preside over testimony of sorcery and devil worship.

The girls flee the courthouse, claiming to be pursued by spirits.

Abigail embraces Mary Warren, who has abandoned her denial of her tales of witchcraft.

Reverend Hale (Rob Campbell) and Reverend Parris demand the truth from Ruth Putnam (Ashley Peldon).

The Salem people, including Ann Putnam (Frances Conroy), and Thomas and Ruth Putnam, cheer another execution.

Setting up an outside shot on the Hog Island, Massachusetts, set of *The Crucible.*

Villagers accused of witchcraft languish in the women's jail.

Elizabeth Proctor comforts fellow prisoner Martha Corey (Mary Pat Gleason).

The condemned John Proctor begs forgiveness of his wife, Elizabeth.

Judge Danforth praises Proctor's decision to confess, and thus save his own life.

Proctor refuses to sign his name to the false confession.

Proctor, Rebecca Nurse (Elizabeth Lawrence), and Martha Corey are taken to the gallows.

Director Nicholas Hytner consults with Arthur Miller.

ABOVE AND RIGHT:
Nicholas Hytner

Paul Scofield
and Arthur
Miller confer.

ELIZABETH: John, you are not open with me. You saw
   her with a crowd, you said. Now you . . .

PROCTOR: I'll plead my honesty no more . . .

ELIZABETH: John, I am only . . .

PROCTOR: No more! I should have roared you down
   when first you told me your suspicion. But I wilted
   and like a Christian I confessed. But you are not God,
   Elizabeth!—Let you look for some goodness in me,
   and judge me not.

ELIZABETH: The magistrate sits in your heart that judges
   you; I never thought you but a good man, John, only
   somewhat bewildered.

PROCTOR: Oh Elizabeth, your justice would freeze
   beer.


38. EXT. DAY. SALEM VILLAGE.

*Justice now arrives in Salem in the form of a carriage, flanked by
armored CAVALRYMEN and INFANTRY, which pounds
up to Ingersoll's Tavern. ABIGAIL and the GIRLS obediently
wait with other VILLAGERS outside the tavern.*

*Out of the carriage emerge THOMAS DANFORTH, Deputy
Governor of the Province, and JUDGE SAMUEL SEWALL
of the General Court in Boston. PARRIS, HATHORNE,
and HALE greet them, making introductions to the SELECT-
MEN, the PUTNAMS, and the GIRLS—to whom the judges
are deeply sympathetic.*

## 39. Int. Night. Ingersoll's Tavern.

*The* SELECTMEN, *with* HALE *and* PARRIS, *are seated with* DANFORTH *and* SEWALL, *finishing a meal.* SEWALL—*on the verge of becoming an alcoholic—is never without a glass of wine.*

DANFORTH: —I assure you, gentlemen, that His Majesty's Government is now determined that the Devil shall not rule over one single inch of Massachusetts; and if, indeed, he has come, here in Salem is where we shall dig him out!

> *The* LOCALS *are rapt, awed, excited. Now* SEWALL *gathers himself, raising a monitory finger.*

SEWALL: . . . Provided every precaution be taken to guard against the testimony of distracted persons . . . and, of course, the mad.

DANFORTH: *(Just barely registering the dissent)* Indeed, Judge Sewall.


## 40. Int. Day. Meeting House.

*The first session. The entire community—except for the* PROCTORS—*is crammed into the meeting house. The* GIRLS *are at the front of the court, facing the three judges—*DANFORTH, SEWALL, *and* HATHORNE.

HATHORNE: Bring in Sarah Osburn.

> *She is bundled down the aisle.*

HATHORNE: Now, Sarah Osburn—here is Sarah Good, who has *confessed* to witchcraft, and therefore will not hang. I bid you follow her example; she testifies that when the Devil came to her, you were in his company . . .

SARAH GOOD: *(Interrupting)* Oh, there they stood big as life, him and her! And Osburn writing her name in his book, with her own red blood!

AUDIENCE: *An amazed rumble.*

GOODY OSBURN: *(Approaching the* JUDGES*)* Your Honors, I never see the Devil in my life . . . but I can dance as fast backwards as he can forwards . . . *She throws herself into a backwards jig.*

HATHORNE: Sit down! Sit, I tell you! Sit her down! *The* MARSHALS *grab hold of* GOODY OSBURN. *Suddenly, without warning, she flies over to the* GIRLS, *mumbling something or other. The* GIRLS *begin to groan.*

ABIGAIL: Oh, stop hurting me, Goody Osburn! Help me, Judge Danforth! *The* MARSHALS *drag* OSBURN *back in front of the* JUDGES.

DANFORTH: What are you doing to these girls?

HATHORNE: What do you mumble to make them so sick?

GOODY OSBURN: I was only saying my Commandments! I hope I may say my Commandments!

SEWALL: *(To* DANFORTH*)* Pray let her recite her Commandments.

GOODY OSBURN: Oh, Your Grace . . . I may only say my Commandments outdoor.

DANFORTH: There are Ten Commandments. Do you
know any?

*No reply. All the* GIRLS *are now clutching their bellies
and moaning.*

DANFORTH: You have lied to the court. I say you have
lied to the court, have you not?

GOODY OSBURN: I am innocent to witch! The Devil
knows that!

*Uproar.* OSBURN *is bundled out.*


41. INT. DAY. PROCTOR'S HOUSE.

PROCTOR *reads from the Bible to the* BOYS. MARY
WARREN *arrives home furtively and skitters across to the stairs.*
PROCTOR *looks up, irritated and surprised.* ELIZABETH
*seizes the moment.*

ELIZABETH: She's been to the court.

*He continues reading.*

*And then the fever starts to grip the town.*


42. EXT. DAY. SALEM VILLAGE.

*Goats have broken into* GOODY SIBBER*'s garden. She pulls
a goat to the gate, yelling abuse. In the street,* VILLAGERS
*look at her with hostility.*


43. INT./EXT. DAY. SALEM VILLAGE.

GOODY SIBBER *answers her door to a crowd of* VILLAG-
ERS *and a few* MARSHALS, *who arrest her.*

HERRICK: Mary Sibber, you are arrested on suspicion of

witchcraft. Any compact you have made with the Devil, you must now confess it!

44. INT. DAY. PROCTOR'S BARN.
PROCTOR *hauls hay from the loft. He ignores* ELIZA-BETH*'s pleading eyes; pleading for action.*

45. EXT. DAY. MEETING HOUSE.
*A* CROWD, *fiercely excited, as if at a rock concert, parts to allow in* ABIGAIL *and the* GIRLS.

46. INT. DAY. MEETING HOUSE.
GOODY SIBBER, *convicted, is hauled from the court, pleading innocence and yelling abuse.*

47. EXT. DAY. VILLAGE.
*A cart is passing up the street, past* GOODY BELLOWS*'s house, where she is working with her little daughter,* DORCAS. *Suddenly, the cart sheds its load of logs. The driver looks up at* GOODY BELLOWS *and* DORCAS.

48. INT. DAY. MEETING HOUSE.
*The* GIRLS *are pointing and screaming at* GOODY BEL-LOWS *and* DORCAS.

49. EXT. DAY. EDGE OF PROCTOR'S PROPERTY.
PROCTOR *and* COREY *have tied a log to some oxen.* PUTNAM, *on horseback, yells down to them.*

PUTNAM: I warned you once before, Proctor! That's my lumber! You're in my bounds!

PROCTOR: My land has always gone up through the forest, and I haven't sold any, Putnam.

PUTNAM: It is clear in my grandfather's will! My land . . .

COREY: Your grandfather damn near willed away my north pasture, but he knew I'd break his arm if he tried it!

COREY *chases* PUTNAM *away with an ax.*


50. EXT. DAY. PUTNAM'S HOUSE.

PUTNAM *watches as two of his servants try to start a bonfire.*

GEORGE JACOBS, *an old arthritic man, passes and waves cheerily. The fire suddenly flares up. Close-up on* PUTNAM's *face—a mixture of surprise and avidity.*


51. INT. DAY. MEETING HOUSE.

GEORGE JACOBS *is seated in a chair in front of the* JUDGES. *The* CONGREGATION *is aflame with suppressed excitement.*

*We see that* MARY WARREN, *seated next to* ABIGAIL, *is putting away a rag doll she has been sewing.*

HATHORNE: Now, Ruth Putnam—where last did you see Mr. Jacobs?

RUTH PUTNAM: He come to me two nights past when I was abed.

JACOBS: *(Amazed)* Ruth!—You are mistaken! You

know me—I am Mr. Jacobs, your neighbor. *(To* HA-THORNE*)* I have six hundred acres next to theirs; she has known me all her life!

RUTH PUTNAM: He come through my window . . . And then he lay down upon me . . . I could not take breath—his body crush heavy upon me. And he say in my ear, "Ruth Putnam, I will have your life if you testify against me in court."

DANFORTH: What say you to this charge, Mr. Jacobs?

JACOBS: Why, Your Honor, I must have these sticks to walk with, how may I come through a window . . .

HATHORNE: But you could have sent out your spirit through a window, could you not?

PUTNAM, *wide-eyed at imminent victory.* RUTH PUTNAM *rushes to* DANFORTH *and whispers into his ear, as* . . .

JACOBS: But how may my spirit go out of my body and I know nothing about it?

DANFORTH: Ruth Putnam has informed me that there is a black man whispering in your ear at this very instant!

*Amazed,* JACOBS *looks around himself. The* GIRLS *start pointing at him.*

ABIGAIL: I see him! He's at his ear! The Devil is here!

RUTH PUTNAM: He's there! He's whispering!

OTHER GIRLS: I see him! He's there! The black man! [Etc.]

*The* GIRLS *faint to the floor.*

*Now* MARTHA COREY *stands up and lets out a loud mocking laugh.*

HERRICK: How dare you mock them, Martha Corey!

MARTHA: What else are fools good for?

OTHERS *join, yelling "Shame!" "God forgive you, Martha Corey!" after she starts for the exit door, shaking her head.* COREY, *after momentary hesitation, rises and catches up with her. The pandemonium grows.*

*Now* REBECCA *and* FRANCIS NURSE *rise and make their way out. People are astonished that the sainted* REBECCA *is deserting the ship.* HALE *looks on, troubled.*

52. INT. DUSK. PROCTOR'S HOUSE.

*Suddenly, as out of air,* MARY WARREN *enters the house.*

PROCTOR *is waiting.*

PROCTOR: How do you dare go to Salem again when I forbade you!

*He seizes a whip and stands.* MARY WARREN *bolts out of the house.*

53. EXT. DUSK. PROCTOR'S HOUSE.

PROCTOR *chases* MARY WARREN *into the front yard.*

PROCTOR: Stay where you are!

MARY WARREN: No, don't hurt me! I am sick!—Pray hurt me not!

*She breaks down, weeping; her genuineness stops him.*

PROCTOR: Get in the house. Go on!

*She gets up, producing a rag doll, a "poppet," as she moves to* ELIZABETH.

MARY WARREN: I made a gift for you today, Goody Proctor.

ELIZABETH: Why, thank you. It is a fair poppet.

MARY WARREN: We must all love each other now.

PROCTOR: Go on in.

ELIZABETH *is mystified by this, and nods and takes the poppet.* MARY WARREN *starts toward the house but again breaks down into helpless sobbing.* ELIZABETH *goes to her.*

ELIZABETH: What ails you, child?

MARY WARREN: Oh, Mr. Jacobs will hang!

PROCTOR: Hang!

MARY WARREN: Aye, and Goody Osburn too.

PROCTOR: The Deputy Governor will permit it?

MARY WARREN: He must. But not Sarah Good—she will only sit in jail some time. For Sarah Good confessed, y'see.

ELIZABETH *stares at her in fear.* MARY WARREN *looks from her to* PROCTOR, *realizes their disbelief.*

MARY WARREN: I am amazed you do not see the weighty work we do! The Devil is loose in Salem, Mr. Proctor; we must discover where he's hiding! *(Gathering her courage)* So I'll be gone every day for some time. I am an official of the court now . . .

PROCTOR *raises his whip.*

PROCTOR: I'll thrash the Devil out of you!

*Whip in hand, he chases after her, grabs her.*

MARY WARREN: *(Pointing at ELIZABETH)* No! No! I saved her life tonight!

ELIZABETH *leaps to her feet, her premonitions confirmed.* PROCTOR *releases* MARY WARREN; *he and* ELIZABETH *stand stunned.*

ELIZABETH: I am accused?

MARY WARREN: You were somewhat . . . mentioned. But I told the court I never see no sign you ever sent your spirit out to hurt no one, and they dismissed it.

ELIZABETH: Who accused me?

MARY WARREN: I am bound by law, I cannot tell.

ELIZABETH *moves, staring in calculation, fear.*

*She goes into the house.*

PROCTOR: Go to bed, Mary.

MARY WARREN: I'll not be ordered to bed no more, Mr. Proctor! I am eighteen and a woman, however single!

PROCTOR: You wish to sit up? Then sit up.

MARY WARREN: I wish to go to bed!

PROCTOR: Good night then!

MARY WARREN: Good night.

*She stomps inside.* PROCTOR *follows.*


54. INT. DUSK. PROCTOR'S HOUSE.

ELIZABETH, *pacing the room as* PROCTOR *enters, clutches the poppet.*

ELIZABETH: The noose is up!

PROCTOR: There'll be no noose.

ELIZABETH: Abigail wants me dead, John. You know it.

> *She puts the poppet on a shelf and goes upstairs. PROC-TOR is burning with guilt as he looks after his wife.*

## 55. EXT. DAY. INGERSOLL'S TAVERN.

*The next day, ABIGAIL accepts DANFORTH's thanks. As she heads across the street to the Parris house with PARRIS and BETTY, suddenly her attention is caught.*

*From her point of view, we see PROCTOR on horseback at the top of the street, looking at her. He turns and rides toward the forest.*

## 56. EXT. DAY. FOREST.

*ABIGAIL runs into a clearing, where PROCTOR is waiting alone.*

PROCTOR: I come to tell you to think on what to do to save yourself.

> *No response from ABIGAIL.*

PROCTOR: You will say you are blind to spirits; you cannot see them anymore, and you will never cry witchery again.

ABIGAIL: I know you must speak so, John, I understand; but my spirit's changed entirely. I suffer now.

> *PROCTOR laughs with contempt and disbelief.*

ABIGAIL: It's the truth, John. Look, the bite your wife gave me's not yet healed.

PROCTOR: My wife?

ABIGAIL: Saturday—she come into my bed in the middle of the night and bite at my breast!

PROCTOR: My wife has not left the house this month!

ABIGAIL: Why must she leave the house to send her spirit on me? Don't George Jacobs come jabbin' at me with his walking sticks?—Feel the lumps he give me only last night!

*She pulls his hand against her thigh, and he withdraws it.*

PROCTOR: George Jacobs is locked up in the jail.

ABIGAIL: And thank God he is! They're going to hang him, you know. And he prays, you know, he prays in jail!

PROCTOR: May he not pray?

ABIGAIL: And torture me at night while he's praying in the jail? That hypocrite!—But they all are, and thank God I have the power to cleanse the town of them!

*He pins her up against a tree.*

PROCTOR: Hear me—if ever you cry witch against my wife it will be the end of you. I will not have her condemned.

ABIGAIL: *(Incredulous)* I am but God's finger, John; if He would condemn Elizabeth, she would be condemned.

PROCTOR: *(Leans close to her face)* You know me—if she is condemned it will be the end of you.

*PROCTOR violently pushes her away and departs. We stay with her for a moment; her eyes are fearful, but a determination flows over her face.*

57. INT. DAY. INGERSOLL'S TAVERN.

*In the doorway is* ABIGAIL, *who staggers helplessly into the tavern parlor, clutching her belly and moaning loudly. She lifts her bodice and draws a long needle from her stomach. She looks at the* JUDGES, *crying.*


58. EXT. DAY. INGERSOLL'S TAVERN.

DANFORTH *and* SEWALL *watch as* HERRICK, *now appointed marshal, is cracking a whip over a team of oxen that begin drawing a long open wagon; there are chains hanging from stakes spaced along its sides.* CHEEVER *is seated beside* HERRICK, *and some* CAVALRY *depart with them.*

DANFORTH: Samuel, I believe you are sometimes not entirely content with us, am I correct?

SEWALL: *(Hesitates a moment, then decides to speak)* I must tell you, Thomas—I had not expected so much of our evidence to come from children . . . had you?

DANFORTH: *(Unwillingly)* I had not. But you cannot doubt the children are painfully attacked?

SEWALL: No, I see that plainly.

DANFORTH: Recall the Gospel, Samuel—"From the mouths of babes shall come the truth . . ."

SEWALL: Aye, aye, but it is also this Putnam woman; I wonder if losing her children has not distracted her mind. And Mr. Putnam—I learn that he is in constant disputation with his neighbors over his boundaries . . . and then there are some . . . *(Daring to say it)* who tell me he is not honest.

DANFORTH: *(Patting* SEWALL's *arm—both threat and love)* Dear friend, no court can wait for saints to provide evidence. I shall be scrupulously just—surely you will rest on that.

DANFORTH *enters the tavern, leaving* SEWALL *alone, staring after the prison cart.*

SEWALL: *(Under his breath)* . . . I have never doubted that, Thomas.


59. EXT. NIGHT. PROCTOR'S HOUSE.

PROCTOR *is inside the barn, working, when* HALE *rides into the farmyard.* ELIZABETH *appears at the door, drawn by the sound of* HALE's *gig.* PROCTOR *exits the barn to see who it is.*

PROCTOR: Mr. Hale.

HALE: Proctor.

PROCTOR: Good evening to you, sir.

HALE: *(Nods to* PROCTOR, *turns to* ELIZABETH*)* You are Goodwife Proctor.

ELIZABETH: Aye, sir—Elizabeth.

HALE *stares at* ELIZABETH *for a long moment. Then he looks at* PROCTOR *penetratingly.*

HALE: I know not if you are aware—your wife's name is mentioned in the court.

PROCTOR: Our Mary Warren told us; we are entirely amazed.

HALE: I am a stranger here, as you know. And I find it hard to draw a clear opinion of them that are accused.

And so I go tonight from house to house . . . I come now from Rebecca Nurse's house . . .

ELIZABETH: Rebecca's charged?

HALE: God forbid that such a one be charged, but she is . . . mentioned somewhat.

ELIZABETH: Mr. Hale, I hope you will never believe that Rebecca trafficked with the Devil.

*This is exactly what's been troubling* HALE, *so he stiffens and evades a direct reply.*

HALE: Goody Proctor, this is a strange time; none can any longer doubt that the powers of darkness are attacking this village—

PROCTOR: —We have no knowledge in that line, Mr. Hale.

HALE: *(Vaguely sensing evasion here)* —I thought, sir, to put some questions as to the Christian character of this house, if you'll permit me.

PROCTOR: We have no fear of questions, sir. Come in.

*They move to the house.*


60. INT. NIGHT. PROCTOR'S HOUSE.

HALE: In the book of record Mr. Parris keeps I note that you are come to Sabbath meeting but twenty-six time in seventeen month.

PROCTOR: Sit down, Mr. Hale . . . I will be straight with you; no minister before him ever demanded the deed to the house we lend him. And since we built the meeting house there were pewter candlesticks upon the pulpit; but Parris came, and week after week preach nothing but golden candlesticks until he had them. I'll not deny it, sir, when I look to Heaven and see my money glaring at his elbows, it hurt my prayer, sir, it hurt my prayer.

HALE: . . . And your children—how comes it the last is not baptized?

PROCTOR: *(Dreading he is getting in deeper)* I . . . like it not that Mr. Parris lay his hand on my baby. I'll not conceal it, sir, I see no light of God in that man.

HALE: The man's ordained, therefore the light of God is in him.

PROCTOR: *(Angered now)* What's your suspicion, Mr. Hale?—I nailed the roof upon the church, I hung the door . . .

HALE: That's a good sign . . .

ELIZABETH: Maybe we are too hard on Parris, but sure we never loved the Devil here.

HALE: . . . Do you know your Commandments, Elizabeth?

ELIZABETH: I surely do—I am convenanted, sir. There be no mark upon my Christian life.

HALE: And you, Mister?

PROCTOR: Aye, I am sure I do.

HALE: Let you repeat them, if you will.

PROCTOR: My Commandments?

HALE: Aye.

PROCTOR: Thou shalt not kill. Thou shalt not steal.

Thou shalt not covet thy neighbor's goods, nor make unto thee any graven image. Thou shalt not take the name of the Lord in vain; thou shalt have no other gods before me. *(Starting to falter)* Thou shalt remember the Sabbath Day and keep it holy. *(Pause)* Thou shalt honor thy father and mother; thou shalt not bear false witness. *(He is stuck.)* Thou shalt not make unto thee any graven . . .

HALE: You have said that twice.

PROCTOR: I know. *(Lost, eyes desperate)*

ELIZABETH: Adultery, John.

PROCTOR: Aye!—Aye, you see, between the two of us we do know them all. I think it be a small fault.

HALE: Theology, sir, is a fortress; no crack in a fortress may be accounted small. I bid you both good night, then . . .

*He leaves the house.* ELIZABETH *watches him go, then gets up and hurries after him.*


61. EXT. NIGHT. PROCTOR'S HOUSE.

HALE *is about to mount his gig when* ELIZABETH *calls from the door.*

ELIZABETH: Mr. Hale?

HALE *turns to her. She turns to* PROCTOR, *who comes beside her. He is erect, prepared for the onslaught.*

PROCTOR: Mr. Hale . . . I know the children's sickness had naught to do with witchcraft.

HALE *reacts with total alertness—he has suspected this himself, but the Devil could be tricking him now.*

HALE: What's that?

PROCTOR: Mr. Parris—he discovered them sportin' in the woods. They were startled and took sick.

HALE: Who told you this?

PROCTOR: *(The name dries his mouth.)* Abigail Williams.

HALE: . . . *Abigail Williams* told you it had naught to do with witchcraft?

PROCTOR: She told me the night you came, sir.

HALE: Why did you keep this?

PROCTOR: I never knew till tonight that the world has gone mad with all this nonsense.

HALE: Mister, I have myself examined Tituba, Sarah Good, and twenty-six others who have confessed to dealing with the Devil. They've *confessed* it!

PROCTOR: And why not, if they must hang for denying it? Have you ever thought of that?

HALE: *(Turning to* ELIZABETH*)* I have a rumor you do not believe there are witches in the world. Is that true?

PROCTOR: *(Waffling)* . . . Well, the Bible speaks of witches, so . . .

ELIZABETH: Sir, I am a good woman. I know it. If you believe that I may only do good work in the world and yet be secretly bound to Satan, then I must tell you I do not believe it.

PROCTOR: You bewilder him.

HALE: *(Frightened)* But you do believe there are witches . . .

ELIZABETH: If he think I am one, then I say there are none!

HALE: You surely do not fly against the Gospels . . .

ELIZABETH: *(Snapping out of control)* Question Abigail Williams about the Gospels, not myself!

*They are turned by the sound of horses' hoofs. Two old men gallop up to a stop. From the wagon . . .*

COREY: John! John! They've taken my Martha . . . and Rebecca!

HALE: Taken Rebecca! On what charge?

NURSE: "For the supernatural murder of Goody Putnam's babies!"

PROCTOR: *(Furiously to HALE)* Rebecca Nurse have murdered children, Mr. Hale? Are you still believing this?

HALE: *(Desperately hanging on)* Remember . . . until an hour before the Devil fell, God thought him beautiful in Heaven!

*From a distance the sound of a heavy wagon startles them. A moment of dread. A swinging lantern is seen, then a wagon, on which sit CHEEVER, HERRICK, MAR-SHALS, and SIX PRISONERS—including MAR-THA and REBECCA, all chained.*

NURSE: Oh, my dear Rebecca!

COREY: We'll soon have you free, Martha!

MARTHA: Pity Cheever, not us—he's the one is going to Hell!

CHEEVER: Good evenin' to you, Proctor—all.

PROCTOR: Cheever.

CHEEVER: I have a warrant for your wife.

> PROCTOR, *outraged, looks to* HALE.

HALE: I know nothing of this. Who charged her?

CHEEVER: Why, Abigail Williams charge her.

PROCTOR: For what crime, on what proof?

CHEEVER: I like not to search a man's house, but by law I must enter.

## 62. INT. NIGHT. PROCTOR'S COMMON ROOM.

ELIZABETH *is standing, waiting.* CHEEVER *and the* OTHERS *enter.*

CHEEVER: Will you hand me any poppets that your wife may keep here?

ELIZABETH: I have kept no poppets since I were a girl.

> CHEEVER *stares persistently at a point; all turn to look. On the mantel is the poppet* MARY WARREN *brought for* ELIZABETH.

ELIZABETH: Oh! *(Goes to fetch it)* This is Mary's . . .

PROCTOR: Mary, come down here! Mary!

> CHEEVER *holds out his hand, and* ELIZABETH *gives him the poppet. Suddenly he pulls his hand away, then lifts the apron and draws out a needle.*

CHEEVER: I had my doubts, Proctor, but this is calamity!

*(Showing the needle to* HALE*)* You see it, sir, it is a needle!

HALE: Why, what signifies a needle?

CHEEVER: The Williams girl . . . Abigail . . . today at the tavern she fall to the floor with a needle stuck two inches into her belly! And she testify it were your wife's familiar spirit pushed it in!

MARY WARREN *enters from the stairway.*

PROCTOR: Mary . . . tell how this poppet come into my house.

MARY WARREN: *(Stalling)* What poppet's that, sir?

PROCTOR: *(Grabbing the poppet from* CHEEVER*)* This poppet, this poppet!

MARY WARREN: Why . . . I made that in court . . . and give it to Goody Proctor yesterday.

PROCTOR *looks challengingly at* HALE.

HALE: Mary, a needle's been discovered inside that poppet . . .

MARY WARREN: Oh, I meant no harm by it, sir.

PROCTOR: You stuck it in yourself?

MARY WARREN: For safekeeping. I must have forgot to take it out.

HALE: Child . . . you are quite certain this be your natural memory—no one might be conjuring you to say this?

MARY WARREN: No, sir, I am entirely myself. *(A bright idea)* Let you ask Abby—Abby sat beside me when I made it.

ELIZABETH: That girl is murder! She must be ripped out of the world!

CHEEVER: You heard that, Herrick—"ripped out of the world!"

PROCTOR *snatches the warrant out of* CHEEVER's *hand and rips it up.*

PROCTOR: Out of my house!

HALE: Now, Proctor . . .

PROCTOR: And you with them! You are a broken minister!

HALE: I promise you, if she is innocent . . .

PROCTOR: If *she* is innocent! Why do you never wonder if Parris be innocent, or Putnam or Abigail? Are the accusers always holy now, were they born this morning as pure as God's fingers? I'll tell you what's walking Salem—vengeance! The little crazy children are jangling the keys of the kingdom, and common vengeance writes the law!—I'll not give my wife to vengeance!

*The two* PROCTOR BOYS *appear on the stairs, awakened from sleep.*

ELIZABETH: I think I must go with them.

*All remain silent as* ELIZABETH *calms* PROCTOR *with a touch.*

ELIZABETH: Mary, there is bread enough for the morning. You will bake in the afternoon. *(To the* BOYS*)* Heed your father. Help him.

BOYS: Yes, Mother.

PROCTOR: I'll bring you home soon!

> *She goes to the* BOYS. *They are open-mouthed and scared; she kisses them.*

ELIZABETH: *(With no belief)* Aye, John. Bring me soon. Be good, my boys.

PROCTOR: I will fall like an ocean on that court! Fear nothing, Elizabeth.

ELIZABETH: I will fear nothing.

> *She then turns and walks out with the* MARSHALS.


63. EXT. NIGHT. PROCTOR'S HOUSE.

ELIZABETH *is mounting the wagon in which the other* PRISONERS *sit.* PROCTOR *watches from the door.* HERRICK *starts to cuff her to a chain.*

PROCTOR: You'll not chain her!

> *He leaps up onto the wagon and pulls down a* MARSHAL. *There is a fight, with* COREY *and* NURSE *coming to his defense and his two* BOYS *joining in; the* MARSHALS *subdue him.*

HERRICK: *(To the* MEN, *pleadingly)* In God's name, John, let me stand to my duty; I must chain them all!

> CHEEVER, *on the driver's seat, cracks a whip, and the wagon drives off.* HALE, COREY, *and* NURSE *follow.* MARY WARREN *lurks in the doorway.*

PROCTOR: You are coming with me to the court to-morrow. *(She turns in alarm.)* You will tell the court how that poppet come here and who stuck the needle in.

MARY WARREN: I cannot charge murder on Abigail.

*He moves. She begins to back in fear toward the door.*

MARY WARREN: She'll charge lechery on you, Mr. Proctor!

*He halts, teeth clenching with embarrassment and anger. Then—*

PROCTOR: My wife will not die for me!

MARY WARREN: I cannot do it, they'll turn on me!

PROCTOR *lifts her off the step by the throat—she is choking.*

PROCTOR: That goodness will not die for me, Mary! I will bring your guts into your mouth but she will not die for me! You will tell the court what you know; make your peace with it.

*He drops her to the ground as she weeps—"I cannot, I cannot do it, they'll turn on me!"*

PROCTOR: Peace!—Now Hell and Heaven grapple on our backs, and all our old pretense is ripped away . . . (With dread he looks straight up at the stars.) Aye . . . And God's icy wind will blow!

64. EXT. DAY. MEETING HOUSE.
*A furious storm lashes the meeting house.*

65. INT. DAY. MEETING HOUSE.
*The house is full. We are in mid-interrogation.*

HATHORNE: Now, Martha Corey, how did you know

beforehand that Goody Wofford's pigs were to die the night of your visit to her?

MARTHA: As you know well, Mr. Hathorne, I have kept pigs all of my life, and pigs that is not fed properly is very likely to die. I had suspicions—

HATHORNE: Suspicions?—You *predicted* the pigs would die, Martha Corey, how came you to know that?

MARTHA: Mr. Hathorne, I am innocent to a witch, I know not what a witch is.

HATHORNE: *(Playing to the AUDIENCE)* If ye know not what a witch is, how do you know you are not one?

*The* CONGREGATION'*s fury is abruptly interrupted by the main doors swinging open.* PROCTOR, *pulling the terrified* MARY WARREN, *and followed by* COREY *and* NURSE, *smashes his way up to* DAN-FORTH. *Wind and rain.*

PROCTOR: Your Excellency!

PARRIS *instantly rushes to* DANFORTH, *pointing at* PROCTOR.

PARRIS: Beware that man!

COREY: We have evidence for the court! The girls are frauds!

ABIGAIL *glares out at* MARY WARREN, *who averts her gaze.* PROCTOR *still has her by the hand.*

COREY: They are frauds! Mary Warren's come back to tell the truth!

DANFORTH: Who is this man?

PARRIS: Giles Corey, and a more contentious . . .

COREY: I am old enough to answer! *(To* DANFORTH*)* I am Giles Corey. I have written a deposition which will open up your eyes, sir!

CONGREGATION *in turmoil.*

COREY: This is John Proctor; he has three hundred acres, and Francis Nurse, sir, with twelve hundred acres . . .

*Meanwhile,* DANFORTH *and the other* JUDGES *abruptly stalk toward the side door.*

CHEEVER: The court is in recess!

*Chaotically, furious* DANFORTH, *with* SEWALL *behind him, is moving toward a door to one side; behind them,* PARRIS, HALE, COREY, NURSE, PROCTOR, *and* MARY WARREN.

66. EXT. DAY. SIDE OF MEETING HOUSE.

DANFORTH *and the* OTHERS *step outside into the rain and head to the tavern.* PROCTOR *drags the frightened* MARY WARREN.

67. INT. DAY. INGERSOLL'S TAVERN.

ALL *are filing into the tavern;* DANFORTH, SEWALL, *and* HATHORNE *are arranging themselves by a long table in the rear of the room.*

COREY: . . . Your Excellency, I never called my wife a witch, I only said she were readin' strange books . . .

NURSE: We mean no disrespect, sir . . .

DANFORTH: Disrespect?—This is disruption, Mister! This is the highest court of the supreme government of the province, do you know it?—Who is this man?

HALE: His wife's Rebecca Nurse that were condemned this morning.

DANFORTH: Nurse? Indeed!—I have only good report of your character, sir—I am amazed to find you in this uproar.

NURSE: Excellency, we have proof for your eyes—the girls are frauds.

PROCTOR *enters with* MARY WARREN, *who seems a total blank now.*

PARRIS: Mary Warren! We were told you are sick. What are you about here?

ALL *await* MARY WARREN's *response, but she is reticent.*

PROCTOR: She has been striving with her soul, Mr. Parris. She would speak with His Excellency.

PARRIS: Beware this man, sir; this man is set and bound to destroy my ministry!

HALE: Judge Sewall, I think you *must* hear this child.

DANFORTH: We "must" do nothing but what justice bids us do, Mr. Hale. What would you tell us, Mary Warren?

*She is tongue-tied, swallowing a dry throat.*

PROCTOR: She never saw no spirits, sir. She will swear to you that none of the other girls ever saw them neither.

*They are all aware that this girl is the ultimate challenge to the government itself.*

PARRIS: And you intend to spread this lie in open court before the whole village?

PROCTOR, *ignoring* PARRIS, *turns to* DAN-FORTH.

PROCTOR: We were sure His Excellency would welcome the truth, as we can prove it, sir.

DANFORTH: *(Out of the blue)* Have you ever seen the Devil, Mr. Proctor?

PROCTOR: *(Startled)* No.

DANFORTH: And there is no desire lurking in your heart to undermine these investigations?

PROCTOR: No, sir. I have come only to save my innocent wife . . . and my friends'.

DANFORTH *now beckons* SEWALL *and* HA-THORNE *to a corner, whispering.*

DANFORTH: What do you make of this?

SEWALL: *(Strongly)* God help me, I cannot say; but I am sure the child must be heard, Thomas, or it will surely spread that you silenced her.

*More whispering.*

HATHORNE: Aye, she's the one.

DANFORTH: Your wife, Mr. Proctor, has sent me a claim that she is pregnant now.

PROCTOR *astonished, half happy and half alarmed.*

DANFORTH: There be no sign of it—we have examined her body.

PROCTOR: But if she say she is pregnant, she must be. That woman will never lie, Mr. Danforth.

DANFORTH: She will not?

PROCTOR: Never, sir, never.

DANFORTH: You say you have no other purpose than to safeguard her; very well—the law forbids harm to the innocent child. So if I tell you now that your wife will be safe until she is delivered—will you drop this charge?

*Silence.*

DANFORTH: She is saved at least this year, and a year is long.—Your purpose is accomplished, Mister.

PROCTOR *can't find words for the moment.*

DANFORTH: Or is your design somewhat . . . larger?

PROCTOR: These are my friends. Their wives are also accused . . .

PARRIS: There you have it! He has come to overthrow the court!—It is all dust in your eyes!

PROCTOR: *(Taking out his document)* Sir, I am no lawyer, but I . . .

DANFORTH: The pure in heart need no lawyers, Mr. Proctor. Proceed as you will, and quickly.

PROCTOR: This is a sort of testament signed by ninety-one people, and if you will notice, they declare they've known our wives over many years and never seen no sign they had dealings with the Devil.

PARRIS: This is a clear attack upon the court!

HALE: Is every defense an attack upon the court?

PARRIS: All innocent and Christian people are happy for the court in Salem; these are gloomy for it! *(To DAN-FORTH)* I think you must wish to know why!

DANFORTH *glances over to* SEWALL, *who looks back at him enigmatically, pained but irresolute.* DANFORTH *holds the petition to* CHEEVER.

DANFORTH: Mr. Cheever, have warrants drawn for all of these—arrest for examination.

PROCTOR, COREY, NURSE, *and* HALE *break out into protests.*

NURSE: I have brought trouble on these people!

DANFORTH: Not if they are of good conscience, Mr. Nurse. You must understand, sir—a person is either with this court or against it, there be no road between. This is a new time, a precise time; we live no longer in the dusky afternoon when evil mixed itself with good and befuddled the world. Now, by God's grace, the good folk and the evil entirely separate! I hope you will find your place with us.

*Prompted by* PROCTOR, COREY *reaches a paper before* DANFORTH. DANFORTH *is clearly impressed by what he reads and looks over to* COREY, *then* . . .

DANFORTH: Mr. Herrick, find Mr. Putnam and bring him here to me.

HERRICK *goes out.* DANFORTH *turns to* COREY.

DANFORTH: This is very well phrased; you have no legal training?

COREY: I have the best, sir—I am thirty-three time in

court in my life. And always plaintiff, too. Your father tried a case of mine—might be thirty-five year ago, I think.

DANFORTH: Did he?

COREY: He never spoke to you of it?

DANFORTH: (Amused) No, I'm afraid I cannot recall it.

COREY: That's strange—he give me five pound damages . . .

DANFORTH: Did he!—Well done!

PUTNAM enters with HERRICK. PUTNAM looks about with a defensive anger.

DANFORTH: Mr. Putnam, we have an accusation by Mr. Corey against you. He states that you prompted your daughter to cry witchery upon George Jacobs so that you might buy up his forfeited land.

PUTNAM: It is a lie.

COREY: This man is killing his neighbors for their land!

DANFORTH: But where is your proof?

COREY: (Pointing to his deposition) The proof is there! The day his daughter cried out on Jacobs, he was heard to say he bid her do it!—I have it from an honest man who was there when he said it!

HATHORNE: And the name of this man?

COREY: (Taken aback) Why, I . . . I cannot give you his name.

DANFORTH: Then I shall have no choice but to arrest you for contempt of court, do you know that?

COREY: This is a hearing; you cannot clap me for contempt of a hearing!

DANFORTH: Ah, it is a proper lawyer! Very well.

DANFORTH *briskly leads the* COMPANY *out of the*
*tavern—*

68. INT. DAY. MEETING HOUSE.

*—into the now empty meeting house.*

DANFORTH: Mr. Corey, the court is now in session.

69. INT. DAY. INGERSOLL'S TAVERN.

*In the melee,* MARY WARREN *has been left alone in the*
*tavern. She has her hands clasped to Heaven, and is rocking back*
*and forth.*

MARY WARREN: Oh, my God, hold me in Thy hand.

*Suddenly,* ABIGAIL, MERCY, *and the other* GIRLS
*are in the room, moving toward her, staring at her pene-*
*tratingly.*

MARY WARREN: No!

MARY WARREN *flees in fear to the meeting house.*
*The* GIRLS *stare after her.*

70. INT. DAY. MEETING HOUSE.

PROCTOR *goes to and comforts* MARY WARREN *as she*
*enters the meeting house. A full-fledged fight is going on.*

HALE: Excellency, it is understandable that he conceal the
man's name—there is prodigious fear of this court in
the country!

DANFORTH: No uncorrupted man may fear this court!
—None! Giles Corey, you are under arrest in contempt. Now decide; either you give me the man's
name who accuses Mr. Putnam, or you will sit in jail
until you be forced to answer our questions.—Mr.
Proctor, what more do you have for us?

COREY: I'll cut your throat, Putnam! I'm not done with
you! I'll kill you!

COREY *makes a rush for* PUTNAM, *and as* PROC-
TOR, PARRIS, *and* HERRICK *jump in, there is a
brawl.*

DANFORTH: Remove him!

PROCTOR *and* HERRICK *subdue* COREY, *who
calls as he is dragged out*—

COREY: Say no more, John, he means to hang us all!

PROCTOR: *(Brandishing the deposition)* Have no fear,
Giles, this will bring you home!

PROCTOR *lays the deposition before* DANFORTH.

PROCTOR: Mary Warren's deposition, sir. She swears
upon her immortal soul that she lied and her friends
lie now—they never saw Satan and no witch ever
hurt them. And this is the truth, sir.

DANFORTH *for the first time seriously reads the
deposition.*

HALE: Excellency, clearly this goes to the heart of the
matter.

DANFORTH *turns to him, admitting as much.*

HALE: In God's name, sir—a claim so weighty cannot be

argued by a farmer; send him home and let him return with a lawyer.

DANFORTH: Now look you, sir . . .

HALE: I have signed seventeen death warrants! *This* argument you must let lawyers present to you!

DANFORTH: *(Cool, hardened)* For a man of such terrible learning, you are most bewildered, Mr. Hale—do forgive me. I have been forty-two year at the bar, and were *I* called to defend these people, I promise you I should be confounded. Consider now . . . *(To* ALL, *relishing the clean symmetry of it all)* In an ordinary crime, witnesses are called to prove guilt or innocence. But witchcraft is an invisible crime; therefore who may witness it? The witch and, of course, the victim. Now we cannot expect the witch to accuse herself, can we? Therefore we may only rely upon her victims!—And the children certainly testify! Therefore, what is left for a lawyer to bring out?

HALE: But this one claims the girls are not truthful . . .

DANFORTH: But that is precisely what I am about to consider. What more may you ask of me? Mr. Herrick, bring the children here.

HERRICK *goes out, as* . . .

PARRIS: I should like to question Mary.

DANFORTH: *(Sudden, furious outburst)* Will you be silent!

PARRIS *is shocked. There is a knock at the door.*

DANFORTH: Enter!

MARY WARREN *is crying as* HERRICK *brings in the* GIRLS, *led by* ABIGAIL. DANFORTH *indicates a bench for them, and they sit.*

DANFORTH: Children—the Bible damns all liars. *(He looks from one girl to the next.)* Your friend, Mary Warren, has given us a deposition stating that she never saw familiar spirits, and was never attacked by any manifest of the Devil. She claims as well that you never saw these things either, and that you are all pretending. *(Turns to* MARY WARREN *and* PROCTOR*)* Now, it may be that Satan has conquered Mary . . . and sent her here today to distract our sacred purpose. If so, her neck will break for it. *(*PROCTOR *and* MARY WARREN *stiffen in fear.)* . . . But if she speak true—I bid you all, confess your pretense now, for a quick confession will go easier with you.—Abigail Williams. Is there any truth in this?

ABIGAIL: No, sir.

DANFORTH: *(Indicating* MARY WARREN*'s deposition)* The poppet that were discovered in the Proctor house—she claims that she made it in the court, and that you saw her stick the needle into it for safe-keeping . . .

ABIGAIL: That is a lie, sir.

DANFORTH: —Did you see Goody Proctor's spirit and did she stab you as you have charged?

ABIGAIL: Goody Proctor sent her spirit and it stabbed me.

DANFORTH: *(To* PROCTOR*)* If she is lying, it can only mean she would see your wife hanged.

PROCTOR: She would wish that, sir.

DANFORTH: This child would murder your wife?

PROCTOR: It is not a child. (*To* MARY WARREN) Mary, tell the Governor how she led you to dance in the woods . . .

PARRIS: This man is blackening my name since I came to Salem!

DANFORTH: What is this dancing?

PROCTOR: Mr. Parris discovered them himself in the dead of night! And they have danced there naked.

DANFORTH: *(To* PARRIS—*it is turning into a nightmare)* Naked!

HALE: When I first arrived from Beverly, Mr. Parris told me that.

PARRIS: I did not say they were naked!

DANFORTH: But she have *danced*?

PARRIS: . . . Aye.

*With new eyes* DANFORTH *turns to look at* ABIGAIL.

HATHORNE: Mary Warren . . . *(To* DANFORTH*)* If you will permit me, Excellency . . . *(To* MARY WARREN*)* In the court you would faint when people accused of witchery sent their spirit out to choke you . . .

MARY WARREN: That were pretense, sir.

HATHORNE: But your skin turned icy and pale . . .

PROCTOR: They are all marvelous pretenders!

HATHORNE: Then can she pretend to faint now?

> PROCTOR *and* MARY WARREN *are caught un-prepared.*

HATHORNE: Why not? If it were all pretense, pretend now. Come, turn cold, Mary—*faint!*

> MARY WARREN *shuts her eyes and all are quiet as she tries to faint—but something is indeed missing now.*

MARY WARREN: *(To PROCTOR)* I . . . cannot faint now.

PROCTOR: Can you not pretend it?

MARY: I . . . *(Searching within for a feeling)* I have no sense of it now . . .

DANFORTH: Why, what is lacking now?

> *She is flummoxed, her throat closed.*

DANFORTH: Is it that we have no afflicting spirit loose, but at the trials there were some?

MARY WARREN: I never saw no spirits.

PARRIS: Then faint by your own will. Come, do it!

> *She tenses herself, closes her eyes, tries to collapse, then shakes her head helplessly.*

MARY WARREN: I can't!

PARRIS: Are you protecting Satan? Confess!—You did see attacking spirits!

MARY WARREN: No!—I only thought I saw them but I did not! *(Appealing to DANFORTH)* Your Honor . . . I heard the other girls screaming and you . . .

you seemed to believe them . . . and then the whole
world cried, "Spirits, spirits!" and I . . .

*She breaks into helpless sobs.* PROCTOR *helps her back
to a bench.* DANFORTH *seems to be reached by her
genuine emotion and turns now to* ABIGAIL.

DANFORTH: Child, I must ask you to search your
heart—is it possible the spirits you have seen may be
illusion only, some sort of . . .

ABIGAIL: Why, this is a base question!

DANFORTH: I only ask you to consider!

ABIGAIL: *(Absolutely outraged)* And what shall I "consider"? Have I seen my blood runnin' out of my
flesh, or have I not? Is this my reward for risking my
life—to be mistrusted and questioned and denied?

DANFORTH: Oh, my child, I do not mistrust . . .

ABIGAIL: Beware, Mr. Danforth! Do you think yourself
so mighty that the Devil may not turn your wits?

DANFORTH: What say you!

ABIGAIL: Satan is no respecter of persons, Mr. Danforth,
he may corrupt *anyone*!

*Suddenly she is swung about as though some invisible hand
tapped her shoulder.*

ABIGAIL: I feel the power of Hell in this room!

*She is suddenly looking upward, terrified, and all eyes follow
hers; she begins to shiver. The* OTHER GIRLS *now do
the same, whimpering.*

MARY WARREN: Oh, Abby, no!

ABIGAIL: A wind, a cold wind . . .

MERCY LEWIS: Your Honor, I freeze!

PROCTOR: They're pretending!

HATHORNE: *(Touching* ABIGAIL*)* She is cold as ice, Your Honor!

ABIGAIL: Mary, stop this wind!

DANFORTH: Do you witch her?

MARY WARREN: No!

DANFORTH: Take back your spirit!

> *With a hysterical cry,* MARY WARREN *starts rushing for the door, and* PROCTOR *catches her.*

MARY WARREN: Let me go, I cannot do it!

ABIGAIL: *(Dropping to her knees, arms upstretched)* Oh, Heavenly Father, take away this torment!

PROCTOR: Whore! How do you call Heaven!

> PROCTOR *leaps at* ABIGAIL, *grabbing her by the hair, pulling her to her feet.*

PROCTOR: It is a whore, Mr. Danforth!

ABIGAIL: He lies, he lies!

PROCTOR: Mark her now—she'll stab me with a scream but she is a whore!

DANFORTH: This will not pass, you will prove this!

PROCTOR: *(Watching his life disintegrate)* . . . I have known her, sir. I have known her.

DANFORTH: In what time, what place?

PROCTOR: In the proper place—where my beasts are bedded. My wife, my dear good wife . . . saw her for what she is and put her out on the highroad. And being what she is, a lump of vanity . . . she thinks to dance with me on my wife's grave. And well she might—God help me, I lusted! For this is a whore's vengeance now. (*He nearly breaks down.*) —I place myself entirely in your hands.

DANFORTH: (*Blanched*) Do you deny every scrap and speck of this?

ABIGAIL: If I must answer that question I will leave and never come back, and I will tell the world that Satan has won Salem!

PROCTOR: Your Honor—what man will cast away his good name?

DANFORTH *is head to head with* ABIGAIL *and is looking at her with fear and intense suspicion.*

ABIGAIL: What look do you give me! I will not have such looks!

*As she turns on her heel and marches toward the door . . .*

DANFORTH: You will not leave this room!

HERRICK *steps in front of her. She halts.* DANFORTH *now turns to* PARRIS.

DANFORTH: Mr. Parris, go to the jail and bring Goodwife Proctor here.

PARRIS: Excellency, this is all a snare!

DANFORTH: Bring her!

PARRIS *goes out.*

DANFORTH: Now we shall touch the bottom of this swamp. Your wife, Mr. Proctor—you say is an honest woman.

PROCTOR: In her life, sir, she have never lied.

DANFORTH: And when she put this girl out of your house, she put her out for a harlot, and knew her for a harlot.

PROCTOR: Aye, sir, she knew her for a harlot.

DANFORTH: *(To* ABIGAIL) If she tell me, child, it were for harlotry, may God spread His mercy on you!

71. Ext. Day. Road.

*The wagon is returning from the jail,* ELIZABETH *and PARRIS wordlessly aboard.*

72. Int. Day. Meeting House.

*A tense silence as they await* ELIZABETH. *A rumble heard outside. A pause. A knock on the door.*

DANFORTH: Hold! *(To* ABIGAIL) Turn your back. *(She looks at him in angry alarm.)* Turn your back!

*She turns her back to him.*

DANFORTH: *(To* PROCTOR) Do likewise. *(Glances about to all)* No one may speak or gesture aye or nay. Mr. Cheever, report this testimony in all exactness. *(To the door)* Enter!

CHEEVER *bends to the paper, ready.* ELIZABETH *enters with* PARRIS. *Her eyes search for* PROCTOR.

DANFORTH: You will look at me only, Goody Proctor, in my eyes only. We are informed that at one time you dismissed your servant, Abigail Williams.

ELIZABETH *assents.*

DANFORTH: Why? For what cause?

ELIZABETH *begins to glance toward* PROCTOR.

DANFORTH: You need not look at your husband, the answer is in your memory! Why did you dismiss Abigail Williams?

ELIZABETH: She . . . dissatisfied me. *(Adding)* And my husband.

DANFORTH: In what way, dissatisfied you?

ELIZABETH: She were . . . *(Glancing at* PROCTOR *for a clue)*

DANFORTH: Look at me! Were she slovenly? Lazy? What was it?

ELIZABETH: Your Honor, I . . . My husband is a good and righteous man. He's never drunk or wastin' his time at the shovelboard . . . but I were a long time sick last year, and I thought I saw him turnin' from me. And this girl . . . *(Starts to glance at* ABIGAIL*)*

DANFORTH: Look at me.

ELIZABETH: Aye, sir.

DANFORTH: What of Abigail Williams?

ELIZABETH: I came to think he fancied her . . . and so one night I lost my wits, I think, and put her out on the highroad.

DANFORTH: And did he indeed turn from you?

ELIZABETH: *(Trying desperately to glimpse* PROCTOR*)* He . . .

DANFORTH: To your own knowledge has John Proctor committed the crime of lechery? *(She cannot speak.)*

Answer my question. Is your husband an adulterer?

ELIZABETH: *(Faintly)* No, sir.

DANFORTH: *(To* HERRICK) Remove her!

PROCTOR: *(Crying out toward her)* Elizabeth, I've confessed it!

ELIZABETH: Oh, God!

> HERRICK *bundles her toward the door. The door bangs shut behind them.* HALE *is instantly on his feet, appealing to* SEWALL.

HALE: I beg you, stop now!

> *But* SEWALL, *who agrees with him, can only turn wordlessly to* DANFORTH.

DANFORTH: She spoke nothing of lechery.

HALE: It is a natural lie to tell! Judge Danforth, I cannot shut my conscience to it; I believe this man—private vengeancy is working through this testimony! By my oath to Heaven, this girl is false!

> ABIGAIL *lets out a weird, wild, chilling scream, her eyes turned toward the ceiling. The* GIRLS *turn up, horror on their faces.*

DANFORTH: What is it!

SEWALL: What's there!

> *The whole* COMPANY *is searching the ceiling.* GIRLS *are whimpering in fear.*

MERCY LEWIS: *(Pointing up suddenly)* It's on the beam . . . beneath the rafter!

DANFORTH: What, what is it!

ABIGAIL: Why do you come, yellow bird! But you cannot want to tear my face! Envy is a deadly sin, Mary. Oh, this is a black art to change your shape!

MARY WARREN: Abby, I'm *here!*

ABIGAIL: Oh, Mary—don't come down!

*Led by* ABIGAIL, *the* GIRLS *are climbing over furniture to get away from a point above them from which the "bird" is about to swoop.*

ABIGAIL: Please, Mary, don't hurt me!

MARY WARREN: *(To* DANFORTH*)* I'm not hurting her! I'm not hurting her!

DANFORTH: *(Grabbing hold of* MARY*)* Why does she see you up there!

MARY WARREN: She sees nothin'!

*Now* ABIGAIL *becomes transfixed, staring upward—and all the* GIRLS *likewise—as they fall under* MARY WARREN*'s power.*

ABIGAIL: She sees nothin'!

DANFORTH: Have you compacted with the Devil!

MARY WARREN: Never, never!

ALL GIRLS: Never, never!

DANFORTH: Why must they repeat you!

MARY WARREN: They're sportin'!

ALL GIRLS: They're sportin'!

MARY WARREN: *(Growing hysterical, stamping her feet)* Abby, stop it!

ALL GIRLS: Abby, stop it!

MARY WARREN: Stop it!

ALL GIRLS: Stop it!

MARY WARREN: *(At the top of her lungs, raising her fists)* Stop it!!

ALL GIRLS: *(Miming her, raising their fists)* Stop it!!
*Utterly confounded,* MARY WARREN *whimpers help-lessly; the* GIRLS *mimic her whimpering. She moves, they move.* DANFORTH *looks on with wonder and terror.*

DANFORTH: *(Perceiving a new, dreadful angle)* What brought you to this turnabout, Mary Warren?—Has the Devil got to you?
MARY WARREN *is terrified, now that he seems to believe the* GIRLS.

PROCTOR: God damns all liars, Mary!

DANFORTH: Have you made compact with the Devil to destroy this investigation?

PROCTOR: *(Sensing her weakening)* Mary, hold to the truth!
*She is shaking her head, dumb.* DANFORTH *turns her roughly to face him.*

DANFORTH: What has brought this change in you! You have made compact with the Devil, have you not?

ABIGAIL: She's spreading her wings! She's walking the beam.
ABIGAIL *suddenly points upward.* EVERYONE *is searching the upper air, ceiling, beams.*

ABIGAIL: LOOK OUT, SHE'S COMING DOWN!

*The* GIRLS, *shielding their heads as though a bird were pecking at them, rush out of the meeting house, with the whole mob after them.*

## 73. EXT. DAY. MEETING HOUSE.

*A mass exodus out the front door and into the area before the meeting house, led by the screaming* GIRLS. *Unbounded hysteria sweeps the* CROWD *of people who were waiting outside the meeting house, and they run after the* GIRLS, *who rush down toward the sea.*

## 74. EXT. DAY. WATER'S EDGE.

*The* CROWD *struggles to rescue the hysterical* GIRLS *from drowning, as* PROCTOR, *up to his calves in water, catches up with* MARY WARREN. *She wrenches herself out of his grasp and, looking up at him in open terror . . .*

MARY WARREN: Get your hands off me! Don't touch me! You're the Devil's man! I go your way no more, I love God.

*From the* CROWD: *"Hallelujah!" "Praise to the Lord!" [Etc.]*

DANFORTH: *(Now with vast inner relief)* He bid you do the Devil's work?

MARY WARREN: He come at me by night to sign . . .

DANFORTH: Sign what!

PARRIS: The Devil's book? He come with a book?

MARY WARREN: My name, he want my name. "I'll

murder you," he says, "if my wife hangs—we must go and overthrow the court," he says!

*From the* CROWD *cries of shock and outrage. And as* PROCTOR *approaches* MARY WARREN *to plead with her . . .*

PROCTOR: Mary, Mary . . .

MARY WARREN: No! I go your way no more!

HALE: This girl's gone wild!

> *Now turning to* ABIGAIL, MARY WARREN *begins to sob in contrition.*

MARY WARREN: I love God. I bless God. Oh, Abby —I'll never hurt you more!

> ALL *watch with wonder as the errant child returns to* ABI-GAIL's *forgiving embrace.*

> *Now* DANFORTH, *charged with a clear vision, turns with infinite hatred to* PROCTOR.

DANFORTH: John Proctor, I have seen your power. You are combined with anti-Christ, you will not deny it!

HALE: Excellency!

DANFORTH: I'll have nothing from *you,* Mr. Hale! *(To* PROCTOR*)* Will you confess yourself befouled with Hell or do you keep that black allegiance yet? What say you!

PROCTOR: *(Looks out on the breathless* CROWD*)* I say you are pulling Heaven down and raising up a whore! I say God is dead!

> *An enormous gasp of shocked revulsion from the* CROWD.

PARRIS: *(To the* CROWD) Do you hear him, do you hear him!

> *As* HALE *pushes through the* CROWD, *crazed faces of villagers loom up before him.*

HALE: I quit this court!

> PROCTOR *is being hustled away past* SEWALL— *whose look is totally desolated, defeated.*
>
> *And now the witch-hunt reaches its climax, as the community tears itself apart.*

75. INT. DAY. MEETING HOUSE.

*The* CONGREGATION *is rapt as* PARRIS, *in the pulpit, is in mid-speech.*

PARRIS: And having committed the crime of witchcraft —Rebecca Nurse, George Jacobs, Mary Easty, John Willard, Martha Corey, Elizabeth Howe—

> *The condemned are chained at the front of the meeting house.*

PARRIS: —John Proctor, Elizabeth Proctor, Mary Sibber, Hannah Bellows, Bridget Bishop, and Sarah Osburn —are from this church, with all its blessings and every hope of heaven, hereby excommunicate.

76. EXT. DAY. GALLOWS.

*A huge* CROWD, *filled with excitement and hostility, is gathered for* GOODY OSBURN's *execution—and hurls insults at her as she is to be hanged.*

GOODY OSBURN: No, I'm innocent.

GOODY SIBBER *is screaming her innocence at the top of her lungs as she is to be hanged. The* CROWD *roars.*

GOODY SIBBER: I am no witch!—You'll all burn in Hell!

GEORGE JACOBS *hangs. The* CROWD *roars.*

THREE MORE *hang . . . and more. The* CROWD *roars.*


77. EXT. DAY. SHORE.

COREY *lies amidst the rocks, his arms and legs tied to stakes. Nearby,* PARRIS *looks on with* CHEEVER. TWO MEN *lay stones on* COREY*'s chest. As another large one is lowered on him, he groans.*

CHEEVER: Purge your contempt, and give us the name of the man that accused Putnam. You will say it, Corey!

COREY *stares up at* PARRIS.

PARRIS: Speak man, we cannot relent! What say you, Corey!

COREY: More weight!

PARRIS *straightens, fear and anger on his face.*

PARRIS: *(To the* TWO MEN*)* —Lay on.

But the TWO MEN *hesitate, frightened by* COREY*'s courage.*

PARRIS: Your are commanded by the court—lay on!

*A big boulder is set on* COREY. *A gigantic final sigh escapes him. The scared eyes of the* MEN *at this transcendent defiance and the faith that must lie behind it.*

78. EXT. DAY. GALLOWS.

THREE MORE *are hanging, but the* CROWD *has lost its energy.*

79. EXT. DAY. PROCTOR'S HOUSE.

ABIGAIL *stands alone in the deserted yard.* HALE *rides toward the house on horseback. He stares at her.*

80. INT. DAY. INGERSOLL'S TAVERN.

ABIGAIL *is seated by the fire.* DANFORTH *is facing her.* SEWALL, *drinking nearby, keeps glancing fearfully over at her.*

ABIGAIL: I cannot sleep, sir. A woman comes to my bed every night now and tears at my eyes.

DANFORTH: Can you make out who she may be?

ABIGAIL: I believe she be Reverend John Hale's wife, sir.

 DANFORTH *is taken aback.* SEWALL's *alcoholic stare widens. But* ABIGAIL's *gaze is persistent, challenging.*

DANFORTH: You must be mistaken, my child. The wife of a minister is not likely to be . . .

ABIGAIL: Satan may reach anyone, sir.

 *She rises, mission done.*

SEWALL: *(Suddenly near exploding)* Why then, absolutely no one in the world is safe—is that your meaning?

DANFORTH: You are mistaken, child. You understand me.

 *This first real resistance stiffens* ABIGAIL—*but she shows fear, too.*

81. Ext. Day. Salem Village.

ABIGAIL *crosses the street toward the* PARRIS *house. The same* TOWNSFOLK *who worshiped her now treat her as a pariah. She can tell the end is near.*

TOWNSWOMAN 1: *(Herding her children out of* ABIGAIL's *path)* Come away from her.

TOWNSWOMAN 2: God forgive you, Abigail Williams.


82. Int. Day. Ingersoll's Tavern.

SEWALL: I beseech you, Thomas, it must end now. It has struck the people very hard that so many will not confess. There is a faction here, Thomas, feeding on that news. They are sick of hanging.

DANFORTH: I tell you, Samuel, I shall not rest until every inch of this province belongs again to God.


83. Ext. Night. Parris's House.

PARRIS *opens his front door and sees the dagger that has been flung into the wood. Sheer terror lights up his face as he pulls the dagger from the wood; he looks across to the tavern. In the doorway is a* GROUP OF MEN *staring at him. Resistance is brewing. He hurries off.*
*Camera rises to a second-floor window.*


84. Int. Night. Parris's Bedroom.

MERCY LEWIS, *in a cloak, stands watch in the window, looking down.*

MERCY LEWIS: Quickly.

ABIGAIL, *also dressed in a cloak, breaks open a small strongbox, revealing three or four small money bags.*

ABIGAIL: I've got it!

*She sweeps up all the bags and hurries out with* MERCY.

85. INT. NIGHT. PROCTOR'S CELL.

PROCTOR, *chained, is alone.* ABIGAIL *moves toward him.*

ABIGAIL: They mean to take you this morning. *(No response)* There's a ship in Boston Harbor. It's bound for Barbados. I have money for the guard. *(No response)* I never dreamed any of this for you. *(Tears flow into her eyes.)* I wanted you, was all. *(Silence)* Listen to me, John. I have money . . . we could see tomorrow on the ocean. The jailer will let you go; let me call him. *(No response)* I must board ship, John. Will you not speak?

PROCTOR: It's not on a ship we'll meet again, Abigail, but in Hell.

*She knows she has lost him.*

86. EXT. FIRST LIGHT. JAIL.

ABIGAIL *runs away from the jail, and out of Salem.*

87. INT. DAWN. DANFORTH'S BEDROOM.

*We are close in on* DANFORTH's *astonished, alarmed face as he watches* PARRIS *pace the room.*

DANFORTH: Vanished!

PARRIS: She's run off with thirty-one pound. I am penniless.

DANFORTH: Mr. Parris, you are a brainless man!

PARRIS: Excellency—hear me, I beg you. Let us postpone more hangings for a time. *(This stops DANFORTH.)* Now, these three that must die this morning—John Proctor, Rebecca Nurse, Martha Corey—they have great weight yet in the town. Now, if you let them stand upon the scaffold and send up some innocent prayer, they will wake a vengeance on you . . .

DANFORTH: Then Proctor must confess! Now he must confess!

*He leaps up to get dressed.*


88. INT./EXT. DAY. JAIL.

*Crammed inside the jail are all the condemned women and children, filthy and manacled.* HERRICK *is pulling* ELIZABETH *out to face* DANFORTH, SEWALL, HATHORNE, *and* HALE.

DANFORTH: Pray, be at your ease. We come not for your life, we . . . *(He is at a loss for words)* . . . Mr. Hale.

HALE: John is marked to hang this morning. *(Shocked,* ELIZABETH *inhales sharply.)* I have no connection with the court, Goody Proctor. I come to save your husband's life. Do you understand me? *(She watches him, uncertain of his intent.)* We must help John to give them the lie they demand.

HATHORNE: It is no lie, you cannot speak of lies!

HALE: It is a lie! They are innocent! *(Turning to* ELIZA-BETH*)* I tell you, woman, life is God's most precious gift. No principle however glorious may justify the taking of it. Will you plead with him?—Let him give his lie; it may be that God damns a liar less than he that throws away his life for pride.

ELIZABETH: I think that may be the Devil's argument.

DANFORTH: Are you stone? He will die with the morning! But if he will confess, you shall both be at home tomorrow!

*She looks at him, lost, scared. They turn as* PROCTOR *is led from his cell, manacled, filthy.*

ELIZABETH: I promise nothing, but let me speak with him alone.


89. EXT. DAY. SEASHORE.

ELIZABETH *and* PROCTOR *are alone. In the distance is the jail, and outside it stand those who await* PROCTOR*'s decision.* PROCTOR *indicates her swollen belly.*

PROCTOR: The child?

ELIZABETH: It grows.

PROCTOR: No word of the boys?

ELIZABETH: They are well. Rebecca's Francis keeps them.

PROCTOR: But you have not seen them?

ELIZABETH: I have not.

*She downs a flow of tears.*

PROCTOR: They come for my life now.

*She nods. He shuts his eyes in wonder and pain.*

PROCTOR: I am thinking I will confess, Elizabeth. What say you? If I give them that? If I confess.

ELIZABETH: I cannot judge you, John.

PROCTOR: What would you have me do?

ELIZABETH: As you will, I would have it. *(Pause)* Oh, I want you living, John. That's sure.

PROCTOR: How can I mount the scaffold like a saint? I am not that man. It is a pretense. My honesty is broke—nothing's spoiled giving them this lie that were not rotten long before.

ELIZABETH: And yet you've not confessed till now . . .

PROCTOR: It's only spite keeps me silent, it is hard to give a lie to dogs—I would have your forgiveness, Elizabeth.

ELIZABETH: It is not for me to give, John . . . if you will not pardon yourself. *(He turns now.)* It is not my soul, John, it is yours. *(With immense difficulty)* Only be sure . . . that whatever you do, it is a good man does it. *(He turns, surprised.)* I have sins of my own to count—it needs a cold wife to prompt lechery.

PROCTOR: Oh, enough, enough.

ELIZABETH: It is better you should know me!—You take my sins upon you.

PROCTOR: No, I take my own, I take my own!

ELIZABETH: John, I counted myself so plain, so poorly made, that no honest love could come to me! Suspicion kissed you when I did; I never knew how I should say my love. It were a cold house I kept! . . . Forgive me. I never knew such goodness in the world! Oh, John, forgive me. Forgive me.

*She covers her face, weeping.* PROCTOR *calls out toward the jail, at the top of his voice.*

PROCTOR: I want my life!


## 90. EXT. DAY. JAIL.

*An immediate reaction from those standing outside the jail: "God be praised!" [Etc.]*

HATHORNE: Bring out the condemned!


## 91. EXT. DAY. JAIL.

*A table is cleared;* CHEEVER *is sitting at it with his writing box.* PROCTOR *is brought to him.*

*Meanwhile, the jail doors open as* GUARDS *prepare to bring out the condemned to the cart that will take them to the gallows.*

PROCTOR: Why must it be written?

DANFORTH: Why, for the good instruction of the village—this we shall post upon the church door!

REBECCA *and* MARTHA *are meanwhile dragged out toward the waiting cart.*

DANFORTH: Courage, man; your good example may bring them to God as well.—Hear this, Goody

Nurse.—Now, Mr. Proctor, did you bind yourself to the Devil's service?

REBECCA *and* MARTHA, *now manacled in the cart, look on astonished.*

REBECCA: John!

MARTHA: Oh, John, not you!

PROCTOR: I did.

DANFORTH: Now, woman, you see it profit nothing to keep this conspiracy any further. Will you confess yourself with him?

REBECCA: It is a lie, it is a lie; how may I damn myself? God send his mercy on you, John!

DANFORTH: Now, Mr. Proctor. When the Devil appeared to you, did you see Rebecca Nurse in his company?

PROCTOR: No.

DANFORTH: . . . Did you see her sister, Mary Easty, with the Devil?

PROCTOR: No, I did not.

DANFORTH: Did you ever see Giles Corey with the Devil, or his wife, Martha?

PROCTOR: I did not see them.

DANFORTH: *(Realizing)* Did you ever see anyone with the Devil?

PROCTOR: No, I did not.

HALE: Let him sign it, Excellency—it is enough he confess himself!

PARRIS: It is a weighty name, sir; it will strike the village that Proctor confess . . .

SEWALL: *(His first show of anger at DANFORTH)* Let him sign and be done with it!—For God's sake, Thomas!

DANFORTH *unwillingly gestures to* CHEEVER, *who goes to* PROCTOR *with the confession and a pen.*

*Agonized,* PROCTOR *signs the confession.* PARRIS *claps his hands and closes his eyes in prayerful thanks to God.* DANFORTH *reaches for the paper, but* PROCTOR *snatches it up, and a wild terror and a boundless anger spring into him.* DANFORTH *has his hand out.*

DANFORTH: If you please, Mister.

PROCTOR: No—no, you have seen me sign it, you have no need of this.

PARRIS: Proctor, the village must have proof that . . .

PROCTOR: Damn the village! Is there no good penitence but it be public? God does not need my name nailed to the church, God knows how black my sins are!

DANFORTH: Now look you, Proctor!

PROCTOR: How may I teach my sons to walk like men in the world and I sold my friends!

DANFORTH: You have not sold your . . .

PROCTOR: I blacken all of them when you nail this to the church and they have hanged for silence!

DANFORTH: I must have good and legal proof that you have confessed to witchcraft, Proctor!

PROCTOR: You are the High Court, your word is good enough! Tell them Proctor broke to his knees and wept like a woman, but my name I cannot sign . . .

DANFORTH: Why? Do you mean to deny this when you are free?

PROCTOR: I mean to deny nothing.

DANFORTH: Then explain to me why you will not . . .

PROCTOR: Because it is my name! Because I cannot have another in my life! Because I lie and sign myself to lies! Because I am not worth the dust on the feet of them that hang! I have given you my soul, leave me my name!

DANFORTH: Is that document a lie? If it is, I will not accept it! You will give me your honest confession in my hand or I cannot keep you from the rope. Which way do you go, Mister?

*PROCTOR goes motionless. Suddenly he rips the paper, crumples it up; he is weeping in fury, but erect.*

DANFORTH: Marshal!

HALE: Man, you will hang; you cannot!

PROCTOR: I can. And there's your first marvel, that I can.

*ELIZABETH rushes to him and weeps against his hand.*

PROCTOR: Give them no tear. Show honor now, show a stony heart and sink them with it.

*He kisses her with great passion.*

DANFORTH: Who weeps for these, weeps for corruption. Take them!

*DANFORTH sweeps into his carriage. PROCTOR is dragged to the cart. ELIZABETH is staring after them.*

PARRIS: Go to him! There is yet time! *(Rushing toward the departing cart)* Proctor!—Proctor! In the name of God, confess! Confess!

HALE: Woman, plead with him! Be his helper! Go to him, take his shame away!

ELIZABETH: He have his goodness now. God forbid I take it from him.

*She watches the cart depart.*

## 92. Ext. Day. Road.

*The CROWD lining the road to the gallows is confronted with the burning resolve of PROCTOR, the faith of REBECCA, and MARTHA's defiance as the cart passes them.*

## 93. Ext. Day. Gallows.

*As the rope is being affixed to the THREE CONDEMNED—*

REBECCA: Our Father which art in Heaven, hallowed be Thy name . . .

REBECCA and MARTHA: . . . Thy kingdom come . . .

REBECCA, MARTHA, and PROCTOR: *(Some defiance in his voice at first)* . . . Thy will be done in earth as it is in Heaven. Give us this day our daily bread, and forgive us our trespasses as we forgive them that trespass against us. And lead us not into temptation, but deliver us from evil. *(REBECCA hangs.)* For Thine is the kingdom, the power, and the glory *(MARTHA hangs.)* for ever and ever!

PROCTOR *is pushed off the cross beam, leaving the quivering rope.*

94. *Fade to black and then, superimposed:*

*After nineteen executions the Salem witch-hunt was brought to an end, as more and more accused people refused to save themselves by giving false confessions.*

# Cast and Crew

CREW

| | |
|---|---|
| Bob Miller | Producer |
| David Picker | Producer |
| Nicholas Hytner | Director |
| Arthur Miller | Writer |
| Diana Pokomy | Co-Producer |

CAST

| | |
|---|---|
| Daniel Day-Lewis | John Proctor |
| Winona Ryder | Abigail |
| Bruce Davison | Reverend Parris |
| Frances Conroy | Ann Putnam |
| Jeffrey Jones | Thomas Putnam |
| Paul Scofield | Judge John Danforth |
| Rob Campbell | Reverend Hale |
| George Gaynes | Judge Samuel Sewall |
| Robert Breuler | Judge Hathorne |
| Joan Allen | Elizabeth Proctor |
| Karron Graves | Mary Warren |
| Kali Rocha | Mercy Lewis |
| Ashley Peldon | Ruth Putnam |
| Rachael Bella | Betty Parris |
| Charlayne Woodard | Tituba |
| Peter Vaughan | Giles Corey |
| Mary Pat Gleason | Martha Corey |
| Elizabeth Lawrence | Rebecca Nurse |
| Tom McDermott | Francis Nurse |
| John Griesemere | Cheever |
| Michael Gaston | Marshall Herrick |

William Preston
Rita Maleczech
Sheila Pinkham
Peter Maloney
Dorothy Brodesser
Michael McKinstry
Alex Kilvert
Will Lyman
Karen McDonald
Sheila Ferrini
June Lewin
Dossy Peabody
Ken Cheesman
Michelle Stanley
Lian-Marie Homes
Charlotte Melen
Carmella Mulvihill
Jessica Kilguss
Simone Marean
Amee Gray
Anna Boksenbaum
Mary Reardon

George Jacobs
Goody Osborne
Goody Good
Dr. Griggs
Mrs. Griggs
Proctor's Younger Son
Proctor's Older Son
Man
Townswoman
Woman 1
Woman 2
Goody Sibber
Goat Owner
Joanna Preston
Deliverance Fuller
Margaret Kenney
Hanna Brown
Debra Flint
Rachel Buxton
Lydia Sheldon
Sarah Pope
Ester Wilkens